Wedding dress, white with small flaws

novel

The plot of the story is fictitious, resemblance to living people is not intended, but purely coincidental. No liability is accepted for any similarities in the story with real events or with living people. It's a story the author took from her imagination.

A big thankyou to
Birte Micheels
for the proofreading and the great help to translate

1st edition

© 2020 Leyendecker, Gudrun
Production and publishing: BoD - Books on Demand, Norderstedt ISBN 9783752605365

WEDDING DRESS, WHITE WITH LITTLE FAULTS

novel

GUDRUN LEYENDECKER

1 st chapter

Stella pushes the yeast plaited jeast leaf into the preheated kitchen stove, closes the door with a satisfied smile on her face and sets the kitchen alarm for the baking time to 30 min.

The bell rings with a melodic gong from the front door. Moni, the little black poodle, hurries into the hallway with her tail wagging happily .

The young woman briefly holds her hands under the running water and dry her hands with the kitchen towel which is hanging next to the sink.

She thinks for a moment and raises her eyebrows. Is that already Silvia, who she invited to an sustantial Sunday breakfast? And if it she is there, Stella i calms down quickly. Otherwise everything is prepared: cold cuts and cheese are nicely arranged on serving sats, the small grilled sausages and the scrambled egg are in the hot boxes and the table is lovingly set with a colorful spring bouquet, decoratively folded napkins and chocolate ladybugs adorned .

Stella opens the door and a young man with a large cardboard box gives her a pen so that she can receive the gift. She writes her name in a hurry on the display. Is he expecting a tip? She remembers that she only has secures one banknote left in her purse, but before she finished her consideration, if the can change the money, he already turned around and trudges down the stairs .

Moni runs excitedly besides her when she brings the box into the living room and opens it curiously. Wrapped in cardboard and lots of paper, it reveals a large, colorful bouquet of roses, which blooms are intensely scented. At the bottom she finds a letter which she opens full of expectation . There is only one sentence in machine block letters. "Because I still love you, love Mario".

Oh no! Not that old story! Stella groans. She rather wants to forget the time with Mario. Still, the poor flowers can't help it! She takes a vase out of the broom cupboard, fills it with water, cuts the roses and sorts them into the bulbous glass vessel. The doorbell rings again. Who is that? Hopefully not Mario.

She carefully opens the front door a crack. She breathes a sigh of relief. Silvia stands in front of her with a cake package in her hand.

Pleased, Stella opens the door pleased. "It's good that you are here! I already feared someone else. "

The girlfriend pushes the cake packet into her hand. "And I thought that we are having an appointment ?!"

"Oh of course! But I have just received a package with a large bouquet of roses from the flower service, from Mario, and when the doorbell rang, I was afraid for a moment that he would come after personally. Now I'm reassured and relieved . Everything is ready, and I was looking forward to see you. "

The two young women are going to the small dining area where the hostess has set up the breakfast buffet. After Stella put the cake in the refrigerator and Silvia has washed her hands , the two help themselves to the delicacies.

"So Mario still wants something from you," the friend ponders. "It was a while ago. How long? Two years? "

"Two years and a month. And I can still remember everything very well. Especially the meeting back then, in the little café, when I was waiting so impatiently for him. "

"Right, Stella. I remember that you told me the exact day. It must have been very bad for you. "

" I remember those moments exactly. The sun was shining outside , but inside it was freezing cold: I'm sitting in the corner of the little café and spooning the milk foam out of the coffee cup. What a day! I breathe deeply . Maybe the air can expand my tight chest and free it from the indefinite pressure? Will he come today? He made a firm promise, but can I still believe him? I haven't heard from him for three weeks , not a word. I try to remember his voice to remember, when he whispered in my ear that he still loves me. But there is nothing left in the deep caves of memory. My silent tears washed away everything in the sad, lonely nights, in endless

hours of burning pain. Pain that killed my feelings .
There is only emptiness and desolation . And now?
What will he say? Why does he want to speak to
me so badly? May be he just want to say that it is
completely over? That he realized after careful
consideration he realized that we didn't together
go? Will he stammer flimsy explanations or try to
appease me with excuses? Will he come up with a
lie to justify his sudden disappearance? Something
like this: I had an accident, was in a comatose
state?

Without foam, the brown broth in the cup tempts
you to have profound, gloomy premonitions. He
won't have a plausible explanation for his behavior,
I guess. None that I can excuse, and none that
enables a new beginning. The chest contracts even
tighter. Just at this moment he stands before me , a
timid smile flies in my counter . I am staying on
my seat, without greeting, look at him

questioningly. He sits down, looks at me, takes my hand. I quickly pull my arms back and clench my hands in my lap. Now the big story is sure to come ! "There is no excuse," he begins. "But it was only a short adventure and it means nothing. I am very sorry that I hurt you. But i know i love you. Can you still love me? "

I cross my arms. Has he just opened a lock? Tons of earthening emotions are trying to carry me away: disappointment mixes with sadness, hurt pride with anger, jealousy with hurt vanity, hatred with love.

My voice trembles, whispers hoarsely: "I don't know yet."

"And him?" Silvia looks expectantly in the eyes of Stella. "What did he say?"

"He said that he would give me the time until I was clear with my feelings. After that I got up very quickly and walked out of the café . You know everything else. After a while I moved here to the Venusberg, to this pretty little apartment, and of course I didn't give him my new address. Three months ago I quit my job at the film company in Hürth, and instead I continued working as a costume designer, I found a pleasant job here in Bad Godesberg in the fashionable hat shop "La Parisienne". I'm very happy with these decisions at the moment, I am feeling good . Only in my free time, there is still something missing . I'm still looking for that. "

Silvia helps herself with fragrant coffee. "We could go dancing together once again. We haven't done that such a while. What do you think about that?"

"Not a bad idea, basically. But somehow something else haunts me in my head. You know that dancing is a relaxing pastime, but I'm still looking for something meaningful, something that I'm passionate about. "

The girlfriend smiles and takes a sip of her coffee. "Do you want to take a pottery class? Clay is burned there. Or something with enamel in a hot kiln? No, kidding aside, I already know what you mean. At my work in the kindergarten, I feel it again and how much I can be there with body and soul. It is always fascinating when I can watch the little boys and girls discover the world. When they come to me and tell something in their children's language with shining eyes, then I know that I am in the right place. "

"I can imagine that, Silvia. You have chosen a job where you can feel the joy you gave the kids. I'll have a look around here to see if I can find a part-time job where I can do something helpful. "

Silvia is nibbling on the quark dish. "I think you'll find something. Now you've settled in in your new apartment, and now you can look around and maybe get to know a few people. But, now back to Mario, how do you want to act now? You will surely thank him for the wonderful bouquet, won't you ? "

Outside, the signal of an ambulance sounds . "That's the only disadvantage up here on the Venusberg: the proximity of the university clinic. I hear the sirens of the ambulance all the time. But at least it's good to know that you can get help quickly here . What I do with Mario? He surely still lives in Röttgen, in his aunt's house. I dont know. Actually, I don't have to say thank you. I neither ordered nor expected the flowers. That I just disappeared should have told him enough. That means I don't want to have anything to do with him anymore. You think that I have to thank him for the flowers? "She fills also several spoons of the strawberry junket in a small bowl.

Silvia thinks for a moment. "That's what you do when you get flowers, right? After all, that doesn't mean that you forgive him for everything or that you want to start a relationship with him again. "

"I have to take a little break, at breakfast, I mean. Do you want to come out on the balcony right now? It smells so intensely of spring now. And yesterday the caretaker mowed the lawn. I particularly like this smell of hay. "

Stella leads Silvia to the balcony , watches a swallow circling and continues: "Yes, what you said is not so stupid at all. I will answer and thank him. After all, he has my new address now anyway . What the hell?! That does not mean that I will open the door for him if he ever stands in front of it. You're lucky with Jens! You two don't have such problems. "

Silvia leans over the railing and looks at the colorful flower beds that enclose the terrace in the basement. "A true artist, your gardener here! He understands it, put a colorful picture of a flowering plant that looks like a fancy carpet. Jens and I? Maybe it only works so well because he's working all week. I look forward to him when he comes home on Friday afternoons and he says exactly the same to me. Then of course we've seen us a lot and can tell each other everything. But unlike me, he's a cozy guy. If he had stress all week, then he is happy when we both can spend the weekend together in harmony. Of course, that has to do with the fact that his ex-wife used to cause him a lot of stress. So he appreciates me and I respect him. Yes, everything is perfect with him. Almost everything. The only thing that bothers me is that his first unhappy marriage has made him such a grouch. I don't even speak to him about marriage. But when others ask him about it, he quickly looks for the distance. "

Stella rolls her eyes. "Maybe he has a marriage phobia. But every phobia is treatable. As a rule, a confrontation therapy is used. "Her laughter turns brightly into the garden, mingling with the singing of the birds in the nearby birch.

Silvia answers shaking her head. "Oh, how do you imagine that? Should I put him a ring on his finger when he is asleep or drag him with handcuffs to the altar? "

The two women are laughing together. Stella looks after the moving clouds. "Since moving here, I feel like a whole new life is beginning . I have a good feeling, I think I'll make something out of it."

"A cool wind comes up, let's go back inside!" suggests Silvia. "You also have to try the cake I brought with me. "He's from the café, up here on Venusberg. The cakes in the displays are always very tempting, I noticed that last time. So , if you ask me to come back again to the subject of Mario, I think he has sent on the flowers to announce himself. One day he will be at your door in person , you have to expect that now. "

They are going into the kitchen , unpack the cake and decorate it on a large glass cake plate.

"It looks nice!" says Stella and nibbles a bit of cream that has stuck to the paper . "Then I will have to prepare myself mentally from now on, if that actually means that after the flowers the sender will knock on my door at some point. Can I actually slam the door in his face when he's there? "

Silvia puts the cake platter in the kitchen. "You can always think about that. You probably still have some time. But there is nothing to prevent you from letting him in and exchanging a few words with him. You can suggest him friendship that's what men do if they leave a woman. "

Stella fills the coffee cups again. "If he understands that?"

The friend puts the pieces of cake on the dessert plate. " You never know. I don't think men and women get along on principle. Especially not with verbal communication . We are always speaking about very specific topics that contain a lot of factual information, where Jens and I get along. But wherever feelings are involved, it is going to be difficult. It's often better to look each other in the eye instead, smile at each other, hug or kiss. Men and women both understand that equally. "

The two women are trying the cream pie and a piece of the decorated Sachertorte.

"But now I ate enough for three days," says Silvia for herself. "It's actually strange that you always eat a lot more when you're in good company. Do you remember before? After school or sometimes before, we always bought sweets at the stall where the tram went around the corner. What was the name of this street again? "

"At that time it was called Kaiserstraße, but it was renamed several years ago because there is a second Kaiserstraße in Bad Godesberg and this district has now been incorporated into the city of Bonn."

Stella smiles. "And do you still remember those lick clams that we always secretly ate during class? That was a mess! "

"But it was even worse with the free sweets in the little sachet. But sometimes we put it in our hands and licked it. Or the little licorice bombs, which we glued to the back of our hands like a star, with spit and then licked off. Dear me, what little piglets we were! "

They laugh together and remember some sweets, which you could buy at the small kiosks.

"It's good that we lived through that time together," says Silvia. "So we can't forget anything. And if we meet again in 40 years, we will always remind one another. "

"In 40 years? I'm curious to see what will become of us by then. Would you like to take me another walk through the forest to Waldau?

It's time for a walk with Moni. At the weekend I always go for a long round with her at noon, that's good for her. Fortunately, I don't have a full-time job! I couldn't leave my dog alone for so many hours without a guilty conscience. "

Silvia makes a face. "Oh, today isn't good. Jens wants to go hiking with me in the Siebengebirge today, possibly on the Drachenfels. Then I can work off the cake. He already looked a little disappointed this morning because I met you at the weekend. He said that otherwise he wouldn't have too little time with me today because he has to leave early tomorrow. "

"Yes, of course I can understand that. The next time we prefer to meet on a day when Jens is not at home. What do you think if you get him some of the delicacies here and bring them back? Maybe from the salads and a piece of Sachertorte? "

"A great idea, I'll do it. But first I'll help you clean up."

Stella fights back, packs a few parcels with delicious groceries and leads her friend to the door, where the two say goodbye warmly and with a big hug.

***

2nd chapter

Stella wanders through the forest with Moni and keeps the lead brid., Between the old leaves from last year the birds hop around on the ground looking for food. The first wood anemone showed their white heads in the light of the afternoon.

sitting In the pine branches is sitting a pair of pigeons, whose melancholy calls penetrate Stella's ear. She feels addressed by the loud cooing, it sounds like wake-up calls to her.

The young woman let her mind wander into the past. What was it like meeting Mario? Of course, it was also a mild spring evening, and she and Silvia met on the little mini golf course, which next to the Casselsruhe excursion restaurant invites guests to play. The two young women liked this idyllic place, which attracted the guests between the tall pines and played the first ten lanes with enthusiasm, whereby they only had to write dawn a few points full of mutual appreciation. At the alley with the number 11, where the hole for the golf ball is in a slope with a a maze of small metal fences, the accident happened. Stella swung back hard and shot the ball high into the air with the rocket. Unfortunately, there was a handsome, dark-haired young man on the route who was picking up some pinecones from the last runway that were lying in the way.

It happened as it had to, the ball hit the hard-working young man on the head. Stella and Silvia rushed over to him, asked if he is fine while they could see how a little bump developed on his forehead.

"Sorry!" Stamms Stella, embarrassed. "Shall we take you to a doctor?"

The young man refused. "That's not that bad," he assured her. "I'll put an ice cube on it right away, then it 'll be better soon. That was a good punch, quite spirited. "He held out his hand. "I'm Mario and my uncle owns this mini golf course. Sometimes I help him here. He did not choose this place very favorably under the trees. The needles fall here in autumn, and even in spring there are still a few old cones, as you can see here. Now we just have to look for your ball. "

"Don't worry about that!" Silvia interfered. "We'll find it, you better sit down on a bench in your injured state and rest!"

But he didn't let himself be disturbed, instead he searched the lost mini golf ball with the two young women. Stella spotted him first, Mario only a second later, both of them bent down and bumped their heads together.

The young man groaned slightly, both laughed and apologized to each other.

Mario raised his eyebrows. "I think you're targeting my forehead. I've already had a bump, do you think I'm a devil and should mark myself with two horns? "

Stella was enjoying herself. "I don't know if you are an angel or a devil or something between. I mean, I don't know you. "

Mario looked the young woman deep in the eyes. "Then we absolutely have to make up for that. May I invite you both to an ice cream? "

The two young women looked at each other, nodded with a wink, and accepted his suggestion.

A little later they sat on the garden terrace of the Casselsruhe and ate the sundae with relish, while Stella's gaze roamed the panorama of the Rhine, which was presented to them with the Siebengebirge and the many churches and innumerable houses of the city of Bonn from high up in the valley .

Silvia watched Mario out of the eye corner, he looked steadfastly at Stella and seemed to have his own thoughts .

"You can take it here," said Silvia. "This muffled background noise of the urban hustle and bustle still penetrates up here, but it almost sounds like music from this distance."

Mario startled. "I beg your pardon? Oh, yes, it's really nice here. My uncle chose the place very well for tourism. There are many guests here in summer. Are you up here often? "

Silvia looked at him carefully. "Not so often. We both live in the Endenich district, in a house with almost all student apartments. But the

Venusberg is very beautiful, especially the forests with their excursion possibilities and the garden restaurants. We also love the Waldau, with the animals in the fenced-in forest, the roe deer, the goats and the petting zoo. "

"I like animals too, I would also like to have a dog, but pets are not allowed where I live."

"Neither here in Endnich," interjected Stella. "One day I'll move to an apartment where dogs are allowed. I really want to get one. "

Now she also noticed how intensely Mario was looking at her, she dared to look into his eyes as well and lost herself in his deep gaze.

Silvia noticed that something indescribable was happening to both of them, which was happening in front of her eyes at the moment. An invisible ribbon stretched like a bridge from Mario to Stella. The eyes of the two sank into one another.

Deep inside Stella heard a voice which told her that she had known Mario for ages. She was drawn to him by a magical bond.

"Hello Mrs. Brinkmann! Are you enjoying this spring day too? " A female voice tears Stella from her thoughts back to reality.

The young woman is startled. In front of her stands the parish nurse from the parish of Venusberg. "Hello Mrs. Lemke! Yes, the dog likes to walk through the forest here, here he has a lot to sniff out. And look at weather you just have to take advantage of it. "

"I've wanted to ask you something for a long time, Ms. Brinkmann. Perhaps you have some time left outside of your normal work. I heard that you are not busy all day. "

"That's true. And I was just talking to my friend this morning about looking for a second job or an interesting hobby. Do you have any ideas? "

"I saw you in church the other day. You are quite new to the church, but I still have the feeling that going to church means a lot to you. Is that right, Ms. Brinkmann? "

"Yes, I feel safe in the belief of my religion. I've always been like that. Would you like to hire me as a coastal artist? "

Frau Lemke smiles. "No, we have a nice elderly lady for this position who does her job with love. I can well imagine that you can deal well with children. We are still looking for a supervisor for the children's church service group for six to eight year olds . Would you like to join our team? "

Stella thinks for a moment. "This is a whole new consideration for me. I've never done anything like this before. Do you think I'm suitable for it? "

"I already trust you to do it. In your job you have always dealt with people, the pastor told me. Your job would be to tell the children the relevant Bible stories on Sunday mornings, and then talk a little about their meanings with them.After that the pastor takes care of the rest in the subsequent community part of the service. "

"I'll think about it sometime, Ms. Lemke. I can imagine that it is also fun to talk to children about faith. I think about it, and then maybe we'll just try it out to see if I'm suitable for it. "

"I think you are. You have to be a friend and a person of respect for the children at the same time, then it will work out. Will you contact me? "

"Gladly. As soon as I am sure that this is the right job for me, I will let you know. "

The two women say goodbye to each other, wish each other a good day and part in order to continue on their way in different directions.

Stella's thoughts start moving. This offer would be perfect. A new task that brings her together with people, with hopefully still impartial children who may have an open ear. Children who can be shown the way to faith. She briefly remembers her own youth. How was it in the children's church service? Sometimes a bit boring, but depending on the pastor or supervisor, there were also very intense hours that felt like a guide . Why shouldn't she try that too? It would turn out whether the children were listening to her or were bored.

An elderly couple, hooked to support each other when walking , comes towards her and greets her in a friendly manner. Involuntarily she thinks of her own age. How would she be?

Would she also be able to spend Sunday afternoons with a partner?

A young man crosses their path, but before he moves away , will he jerks and turns his face to her . "You have a good dog," he praises Moni. "I once had a dog that just wanted to chase the birds in the forest. He was from the animal shelter and so uneducated that he cost me a lot of nerves, especially when he wanted to chase other animals. "

"That must have been really annoying," Stella agrees. "I have no problems with Moni. At least not when she's on a leash. Maybe it's a bit of the breed. She is a poodle, they are usually calm dogs. "

" I'm Benno," introduces the young man with blue eyes and dark blonde hair .

"I'm Stella, and you already know my dog ," replies the young woman and looks him in the expectantly smiling face.

He nods and extends his hand to her. "Is he always so well? Or does he plays as wildly as some other dogs? "

"Moni is never really wild. Even when she plays at home, with her little plush toys, her ball and her rubber bone, her romp is limited. I met completely different dogs there. Don't you want to get a new dog now? "

"I don't want to expect that from a dog at the moment. I work many hours a day in the office, the poor creature would be alone for too many hours. Otherwise, this part of the city is very suitable for keeping dogs. Here you can go straight into the green from everywhere. I assume you also live up here on the Venusberg? "

"Correct. For a few weeks in the settlement that was built after the war for the officials of the former federal capital. I like it very much here. "

"Me too. I live there too. On the Kiefernweg, quite far back at the bus stop. "

Stella smiles . "And I live right at the beginning, right in the second row behind the apple alley."

Benno is amazed. "Thats crazy, what a coincidence! However, I've been living there a little longer, about two years. And how do you do that with the dog? How do you manage to go for a walk and your work? "

"At the moment I only have a part-time job. That works great, of course. During the hours in which I am in Godesberg in the morning, Moni sleeps well in her basket. She is quiet, not even the neighborhood is disturbed by barking or yowling. "

He looks at his watch. "Oh my godness! Now I actually didn't pay any attention to the clock. I have to finish a business letter quickly and bring it to the mailbox. It will be taught at 6:00 p.m. and you will certainly know that this is the last time our mailbox is emptied. I would have liked to talk a little bit more about your dog with you. But now I have to hurry, I'm sorry! "

"No problem! I think Moni will be bored anyway if I stay here any longer. Go on, I wanted to go a little deeper into the forest to hear whether there is a cuckoo at the moment. "

He grins, gives her a knowing look and brushes a strand of hair from his face. "I don't have my wallet with me, otherwise I would have looked for the cuckoo with you. And don't forget: if he calls, taps the wallet three times, you'll be rich in a few months. Have a nice Sunday, Stella! "

"You too, Benno! And good luck with the letter! "

They wave to each other again and continue on their way in opposite directions.

While Moni is constantly sniffing and every now and then excitedly wagging her tail, Stella listens attentively to the birdsong. Every now and then she stops and listens while her head rises expectantly to the treetops. But nothing happens, the cuckoo remains hidden for the rest of the walk.

***

3rd chapter

On the evening of the same day, Stella phoned Ms. Lemke, who gave her all the information about the children's service. "We will meet on Wednesday evening at 20:00 pm in the parish hall , to discuss the theme for the coming Sunday. It is about the solution from the letter of the Colossians, 3 verse 13. You can think about how you would like to convey this to the children. Just take an example from the everyday life of the children. You will surely come up with something, and if you don't, it doesn't matter. We'll all talk about it on Wednesday and help each other to develop good ideas. "

"And what is the name of the verse that goes with it?" Asks the young woman.

"Letter of the Colossi r 3 verse 13? I wouldn't have known that by heart either. But I've just looked it up. It called: "As the Lord has forgiven you, so you also must forgive." I think , it can do pretty good stories. "

"Good, if you think so. I have to think about that, it should also be a child-friendly story. But thanks for your message, I will definitely be there on Wednesday. This task of teaching children the faith really appeals to me. I hope that I am able to do that too. "

Mrs. Lemke encourages her. "My knowledge of human nature has never deceived me so far, I believe that you can do that. I wish you a pleasant evening! "

Stella takes the Bible from the bookshelf and looks for the letter from Colossians. She reads this passage carefully and then begins to think about it. How can you bring this topic to children? Maybe she can construct a story in which two children argue . May be something breaks during the contest one of the two children something , which the other kid really liked? Something like this: Thea has a pretty piggy bank of porcelain with colorful flowers. Hanna pushes Thea so hard that the pig falls on the floor and breaks. Both are frightened, Hanna is embarrassed and asks Thea for forgiveness . But Thea is angry and sad about the broken pig. She doesn't want to forgive her friend. Nevertheless, both children wish for the friendship, and hope , that by this argument the friendship doesn't break. At some point Thea has to think about whether she can forgive her friend, if Hanna is genuinely sorry for what she has done. Perhaps is also better to tell a story about a dispute between a parent and a child. Anna has promised her mother to come home on time, at the agreed time. But she has wasted time and is way too late, during which the parents were very worried. There is a clarifying conversation between the mother and Anna, with whom the child sees that she made a mistake. Now Anna asks her mother for forgiveness.

Stella thinks for a long time, it's not that easy to construct something useful . Of course, it also depends on the age group for which this story is to be invented . A six-year-old child will not come home alone often; as a rule, their parents will pick them up. What tells us the story of forgiveness and forgiveness still developing? Actually, that's a topic for young and old people. Stella looks at her own life, Mario occurs to her. She hasn't forgiven him either, no, she just drew a line.

She pours herself a cup of tea and sips it. Everything had started so promisingly. On the same day they met, Mario asked for her phone number, and she had no hesitation in writing it down for him on a small piece of paper right away. She felt as if she was struck by lightning , inwardly troubled and hoped to see him again as soon as possible.

In fact, he got in touch the next day and asked her to meet, this time for a walk without Silvia. Stella felt as if she were glowing with happiness inside and out, at least like a street lamp that lit everything around and could be seen from afar.

She stood excitedly at the agreed meeting point, the cinema in Endeich, the Rex Theater. She recognized the glow of being in love in his eyes too. They greeted each other with a brief hug.

After he had bought the movie tickets, popcorn and a drink, he led her inside the ancient movie theater. There was a romantic movie, and right after the first scenes it had took her hand tenderly. This connection seemed electrifying d, Stella had the feeling that everyone could hear it crackling. The pulsing blood in the veins demanded more. The popcorn bag and the drinks stayed closed. After a few minutes he kissed her, so tenderly, so deeply, so passionately that Stella forgot everything around her. They kissed again and again, thirsty like wanderers in the desert. Both only woke up when the film's credits rolled over the screen.

Mario sighed. "What a shame, I'd like to stay in here with you. But a new film is about to start again, we will be kicked out of this little paradise. They left the cinema hand in hand.

They waked a while in the park and kissed each other, again and again. Just when it was getting cooler Stella noticed that it was quite late and explained to Mario that it was time to return home. At her front door he looked at her questioningly. What does this mean? Did he want to go into the apartment with her? Should she offer him another coffee? She decided against it .

This magical dream of falling in love young should last as long as possible, just not a rude awakening! She kissed him deeply again, said goodbye and wished him a good night. There was a faint regret in his look, but it gave way to a new tenderness. The glow she had noticed in his eyes at the beginning returned. Smiling happily, she waved to him for a long time until he had disappeared around the next street corner.

In the small apartment she falls in her bed, overjoyed, and let the last few hours pass by in front of her inner eyes. She tries to get every kiss a second time in memory and enjoy.

Her cell phone ringed in the middle. She suspected it, she knew it, it could only be Mario.

His voice sounded wistful and tender at the other end. As soon as they had lost sight of each other for a few minutes, he was already telling her how much he misses her. Lying on the bed and staring happily at the ceiling , she exchanged tender words with her dream man until midnight.

When they cut the connection after saying goodbye, Stella lay awake for a long time and tried to understand what had happened. That was great love! Mario is the man of her dreams! She decided that she is the happiest woman in the world and that she wants to do everything possible to hold onto that happiness. Not just for the next time, not just for the next few years, no, for a lifetime.

She imagines a life with Mario. First of all, tenderness and love are the most important. Tenderness and kisses , and certainly once more. How would it be to feel his skin and be caressed by him ? How would it be with him at the first night? She saw a lot of movie visitors and lots of walks, lots of conversations, lots of things to do together. And then at some point she would stand in front of him in a white dress and say yes and very loud and with certainty in her heart .

Yes, even now she was quite sure that Mario was the man of her life.

Stella wakes up from the thought of the past. There is no point in thinking of Mario, she says. It's over, absolutely over. Of course they also had good times, as is always the case at the beginning of every new love. She soon discovered that he liked to flirt with other pretty women, and that offended her. Still, she had always forgiven him for it. How in love she was! She was happy when he had confessed his love to her too!

No, she doesn't want to remember : now, she's fine at the moment. The work is fun, there is a new, meaningful part-time activity and here, on the Venusberg, so close to the relaxing nature, she is happy.

Moni comes to her and gets a few pats, then she lies contentedly in the cuddly basket at Stella's feet . The young woman takes a drawing pad and colored pencils out of the desk drawer.

Perhaps she can draw a picture story from the Bible text, probably a story with drawings is more fun than a story without pictures .

She thinks about something, the blank sheet motivates her. Drawings of children playing on a playground are created. Two children argue, a boy and a girl. Stella calls them Kevin and Kim. The girl sits on the swing while the boy stands by and waits for Kim to let him swing too. But the girl wants to keep shaking and doesn't think about making room for the boy.

Kevin gets angry and goes into the sandpit, where Kim had previously built a large castle in the sand with a lot of effort . Kevin destroys the castle in anger. When Kim sees this, she gets angry and jumps down from the swing and attacks Kevin. But Kevin rushes to the swing and reserves his place. Kim is angry at home, in the meantion Kevin is sorry for destroying the laboriously built sand castle. But he doesn't want to go to Kim, because he is afraid that she is still angry with him. Kevin and Kim, who are usually good friends, don't see each other for a few days.

Stella paints the two children individually, each in their own room. Everyone plays for themselves, both are missing their friend.

But after the holidays they meet again in kindergarten. Kevin overcomes his fear and goes to Kim. He tells her that he is sorry that he destroyed her castle. Kim now has the choice of continuing to be angry with him or forgiving him. She has missed him for the past few days and wishes that he would continue to be her friend. So she forgives him. Both feel good, and now they notificed they have missed each other and how good it is that they are now friends again. The children play happily together. Stella paints two laughing children who are building a new castle with colorful Lego bricks.

Stella is wondering if this story fits right? She folds the sheets of paper and keeps them in a drawer for Wednesday. She doubts a little whether it is a good idea to come along with the drawings on the first day of the meeting. Hopefully it doesn't look like that she's trying to be the center of attention, to attract attention? It's probably not about pictures at all. Perhaps it is more important to tell the story in such a way that the children will have fun during the lesson. The more she thinks about it, the more insecure she becomes.

"Well, Moni! Then we'll both get ready for bed now. Your woolly fur also needs a little brushing. And I also have to check you for ticks. "

***

4th chapter

The next day, Stella comes home from her work in the hat salon , she finds a letter in her mailbox. It's from Mario, and she wonders for a moment whether to throw it away in the trash without being read. But the curiosity is greater, she takes it into the apartment, opens it and reads:

"Dearest Stella, I hope the flowers were nice, and my words are the truth. I love you today, I love you tomorrow, and I will always love you. But please, don't throw this letter away now , because I am writing you today for a completely different reason. I know that you have ancestors from the wonderful city of Dresden. And you told me once that your parents were from the Castle of Dresden. Is that correct? Now you have probably also been informed that some very valuable jewelry was stolen there last year . I suppose that you also made it particularly affected. I know how much you love this beautiful city and that you see it as home as well. I can still remember exactly that you raved about the Dresden Zwinger, the castle, the Frauenkirche and many other buildings, and I even remember the Golden Rider . In the last few days I thougt about you in particular , as I am on the trail of a person who I suspect may have something to do with this robbery. I guess that you are interesting, I still interested in this case and therfore I suggest to meet youas soon as possible. Of course you will ask me why I didn't go to the police immediately, but the matter is really too complicated. Perhaps you don't believe me at all, and you think I just made it up so that I can arrange a meeting with you. But I swear that this is the prey, and my observations, the true reason for this unexpected, sudden and rapid meeting. Of course I have to admit that I would be very happy to see you again as soon as possible. Please don't talk to anyone about it, otherwise it can be very dangerous for me, and maybe even for you. That probably sounds totally nonsensical to you, but please trust me once more.

You know that you are you always in my feelings and thoughts that know you already and will definitely be in my heart forever! I will wait for you there, the evening where we met for the first time. I'll be there at 18:00 pm , and I woult love to see you as soon as you can. I'll be there all evening waiting for you.

I really hope that you are coming tonight.

Love

Your Mario ".

Stella is frozen for a moment . What should she think of that? What was he fantasizing about together just to make sure she comes to a meeting? That can not be true! If he suspects someone of having stolen the jewelry in the Green Vault, then he had to go to the police immediately! Why all this complicated story, everything so secretive? There is definitely something wrong with it!

But what should she do now? Just give him a chance and come to the Casselsruhe, where they first met?

It is certain that it's only a trap. He really wants to see her, he wants to lure her and somehow persuade or surprise her, maybe with roses again or even with tenderness. No, she does not trust him. It's all just a story he made up.

But what if he really knows something? If he's really on the trail of the robbers? Should n't she just go and see what he tells her? Actually, she has enough time to decide and leave when it becomes inevitable.

No, she has to talk to Silvia about it first. Maybe she has some advice. She typed rapidly Silvias number on her phone.

"Yes? Hello Stella! What's up?"

"Do you have time right now, Silvia?"

"Just a moment. I'm just putting the children's lunch dishes in the dishwasher. You sound pretty excited. "

"Yes, and if you hear what's going on, you will understand me. I hope, you sit, otherwise you fall determines just around. "

"Well, wait! So now I've found a place. And now I'm bursting with curiosity. "

"I just found a letter from Mario in the mailbox , he wants to meet me tonight at the mini golf course on Casselsruhe. And he gives a very stupid and for me flimsy reason. "

"Well, he probably wants to see you again and tell you how much he still loves you. Then he will want to kiss you to make you weak. That's very clear. What reason did he give? "

"Do you remember the jewel robbery in the Green Vault of Dresden? A lot of jewelry was stolen there on November 25th. And now he claims that he is on a secret mission on the trail of the robbers. And because he knows that my relatives are from Dresden, he of course says that I'm very interested. What do you think about?"

"This is certainly made up and just a trick to get you to hang out with him. If he knows something, he has to go to the police. "

"That's what I thought, but then again, it sounded too stupid to me to be a trick. It makes me really sad that the beautiful things from the old building are no longer there. And of course I would love to help find the thieves and the jewelry. "

"It's a shame, unfortunately I don't have time tonight, otherwise I would go to Mario's with you.

In fact, you will have no choice but to meet him if you want to find out the truth about his motive. This is really a crazy thing. And what does your gut feeling tell you, do you want to go? "

"Yes, I think I will. Otherwise I'll never find out what's really going on. I can still give him my opinion and leave , because at the moment I feel really strong enough to resist him. "

" That's good, Stella. The best thing to do is to remind yourself of how he dumped you on the way there. "

"Well, I actually broke up with him, but at least I had a good reason. He had another one during our relationship just before our wedding, even if it was supposed to have been just a slip. I'll keep that in mind on the way there though, that's a good idea. Thank you, Silvia, you helped me a lot. "

"No problem, I love helping you. See you soon! Will you call me tonight and let me know? "

"Of course! I don't want to leave you in the dark any longer than necessary. "

The two say goodbye, Stella takes Moni on the leash and leads her outside. The sky has closed, it looks like rain.

"We have to hurry up if we don't want to get wet. Maybe it's a belated April shower now, "she says to the dog.

The dark clouds come quickly, Stella accelerated her walk. When she reached the end of the apple alley, the shower pours onto the dry earth. The young woman quickly escapes under the covered window of the stationery shop. She discovers that she is not the only one who is outside; another passer-by has taken shelter under the canopy. She looks in surprise into the face of her fellow sufferer.

"Benno!" She exclaims. "Did you tell me that you have to work all the day ?"

He looks at her happily. "Hello, Stella! I didn't think we'll meet again so soon. Today I was in the office only in the morning, this afternoon I took some work at home. "

"Well, bravo! Then you could still get yourself a dog if you keep doing it that way. But rememberthat the wether is really bad in winter and it is often quite uncomfortable in freezing cold and winter storms. "

He laughs. "I don't mind bad weather. You just have to dress accordingly. What do you think of sharing your dog, for example in winter. If you don't feel like going outside in bad weather, just give me a call! Of course, that only works when I'm at home. "

It has stopped raining, the dark clouds are clearing. Stella squints in the sun. "So, now we can go again, Moni and I are hungry, we will now prepare something for lunch. Till then!"

He takes a business card out of his jacket and gives it to her. "Here! If you don't feel like getting wet outside with Moni, just give me a call! Have fun working from home this afternoon! "She takes the long run back through the apple alley.

When she arrived at the apartment, she eats the leftovers from Sunday dinner and fills Moni the food in her bowl. She originally intended to revise the story for the children's service, but she feels too restless, too nervous to concentrate on it. Instead, she begins to clean the apartment , and she is constantly thinking about what Mario's invitation for the evening will be all about . She ponders back and forth: is he telling the truth or is he cheating on her? Her thoughts doesn't come to an result, so she has to wait until the meeting.

After feeding Moni and taking her for a walk, she changes for the meeting. Should she dress up or wear very basic clothes? She decides to wear a jogging suit. So she can still claim that she only wanted to do one round.

At half past six she got slowly to the place as she tries to remember how much she was disappointed with Mario back then . That was the day on which they agreed, and he had completely forgot about her, because he had met Elena. Also on the mini golf course with her rich parents who had just come from Mexico. The black-haired, young woman immediately liked the charming Mario. He had explained him explain a lot to her, not only the rules of the game of mini golf, but also various ways in which one could visit the most important sights in Bonn in a single tour without losing a lot of time.

Elena had immediately captured him with her spontaneous, warm temperament, fascinated and cast a spell over him. And when she asked him to go to the hotel that evening to bring her the route planner , she took the opportunity to receive him in a negligee and seduced him with her beautiful body and lots of charm .

Mario had later assured her that it had only been this one night and that the next day he had told her that he was engaged and that this one nigh nothingt. He also allegedly told her that he was planning to get married very soon. Elena then did everything she could to win Mario. She stayed in Bonn for a whole year. But when he no longer wanted to get involved with her, she had finally given up her hope and returned to her parents in Mexico. Shortly before leaving, she visited Stella again.

Her face showed the strength of a good loser. "I congratulate you on your steadfast friend. You can be proud of him. All year long I tried to seduce him again. But he stayed true to you. So now you can forgive him and you no longer need to fear me, because I am looking forward to getting back to Mexico, where I am welcome. I hope you will make up with Mario again, right? "

Stella shook her head vigorously. "No, I can not do that. The day before he cheated on me, I bought the wedding dress with my mother. Unfortunately I couldn't return it, it was a discontinued model with tiny little flaws. At any other time I might have forgiven him, but not on the day when I was floating on clouds and believed I was in seventh heaven. "

"You bought a wedding dress with flaws? That was a bad omen. You shouldn't have done that. A wedding dress with flaws cannot bring happiness. Then everything had to come as it did. What on earth , what were those flaws? "

"Oh, you couldn't see them with the naked eye at all. If the saleswoman hadn't pointed this out to me, I wouldn't have noticed them at all. The upper part was with countless applications decorated. At one point, exactly where the heart sits , the glittering jewelry showed a few irregularities. But you could only really see that with a magnifying glass. For this reason it was also greatly discounted. But that was not the motive for my purchase. I just liked it so much, I was fascinated by the dress. "

"And what did you care about the dress? Did you throw it in the trash or give it away? "

"No. Give away? Giving away such a wedding dress is sure to bring bad luck to the new bride and it is a shame to throw it away, after all, it is still brand new. It's hanging in my closet, and I've already thought about giving it away to a costume rental company or a theater fund. It may be enough for a mock wedding. "

"You are pretty crazy," said Elena. "And you are probably very stupid too. Because if you don't forgive Mario, you will make life difficult for yourself and you will also lose the man who really loves you. "

"You can't understand that," Stella contradicted. "It was just a reallybad feeling and he diappointed me so bad. I can't forgive him for that, above all I can't forget that. "

"If you think that way, then you are very unrealistic. I think almost every men cheats in his life even on his wife. Yes, there may be exceptions, you may be right. But most men get weak at some point. And maybe you will find yourself in such a situation yourself. In that moment you will remember it, and then at the latest you will be very annoyed that you did not come back to Mario, because you still love him, I can feel that. Otherwise you wouldn't be hurt that deeply now. "

"There's no point in bringing us back together now, Elena. And if you came ask me for forgiveness, then I have to tell you that I'm not mad at you anymore, and I don't care what you do. There are just a lot of women like you who just take what they want. But Mario was my fiancé and it was he who disappointed me the most. "

Elena sighed. "You will definitely regret it one day. But do what you want! I will forget the whole story now and start a new life in Mexico. I'll leave my address here for you. When you've made it up with Mario again, write me. Then I can be happy with you! "With these words she rushed to the door with her head held high and in her elegant outfit.

When Elena was gone , Stella was exhausted. Why hadn't she scratched the young woman's eyes? After all, she was the one Mario had betrayed her with. She thought about her feelings. No, she really wasn't angry with Elena anymore. There were probably thousands of Elenas. She just couldn't trust Mario anymore. At some point there would surely be the next Elena, and then what? Her decision to forget him had already been the right one, she knews that now.

And today? Stella listens to herself. Does she still feel something for Mario? Of course , there is still a weakly covered wound, and a lot of sleeping feelings. Maybe it's not that good to go to the meeting point? But Mario may have no intention of winning her back, much less seducing her. So she doesn't have to drive herself crazy. Maybe he's really just interested in the jewel.

In the meantime she has come halfway.

The lights are still on in Café Dombrowski, an elderly woman in a black dress with a white apron is raising the chairs. Here in the café they had often sat and had lemon rolls with their coffee. And it was here where he had proposed to her. It had stormed and snowed outside, it had been a real winter thunderstorm. Inside, a fine scent of gingerbread permeated the cozy, warm room. On the tables, which were covered with white, starched linen towels, were small vases with fir branches, which were decorated with golden tinsel and small red balls .

Mario had pulled a tiny package out of his jacket. She will never forget his smile in his eyes when he gave her the gift.

"It's not Christmas yet, but I still have a present for you, Stella."

"Right, it's not Christmas yet, and it's not my birthday either," she said with a smile. "Should I open it anyway?"

"Yes, open it!" With these words he looked at her lovingly.

Stella took off the ribbon and the paper. The small cardboard box opened easily. A small gold ring with a tiny, glittering stone shone towards her.

"What is that?" Stella looked at Mario questioningly with wide eyes.

"A ring is a symbol for everything that never ends. This ring is supposed to tell you that my love for you never ends. Do you want to accept him? "

Should that be a marriage proposal? A few thoughts shot to Stella's head. She remembered many films in which the men kneel down, hold out a ring to the worshiper and then ask them with languid eyes: "Do you want to be my wife?"

Apparently it was this ring that should say the same thing. Should she ask again if this was an engagement ring? No, better not, that could tear him out of this romantic scene. His shining eyes, his soft, tender voice said enough. And his words sounded like a promise.

"Yes," she heard herself say, "Yes, I will take it with all my heart." She kissed him, tenderly and heartily, without paying any attention to the other people in the café.

Their love forever. Had he loved her too when he went to Elena's hotel? Did he suddenly find himself in a different reality, in a different world? In a parallel world that had nothing to do with this one? In his letter he had written that he still loves her. But wasn't he just fooling himself? Was it possible that he only felt the hurt vanity of a spurned lover that drove him to new conquest?

"There you are!" She hears his voice and discovers him under one of the tall oak trees. "Great that you came."

"Hello Mario!" She tries to keep her voice cool. "You ordered me over here so now you can tell me something about the jewel robbery . Is it true? You are on the trail of any secret? "

Mario nods. "Yes. It's a very complicated story. Come on! Let's go for a walk! "

They are going go to the viewing platform, where a small telescope is set up with which you can look over the city of Bonn, the calmly flowing Rhine and the Siebengebirge mountains behind. The peripheral areas on the mountain slope shine in full color tones, the pastel shades of the Rhine plain and the hilly mountain range of the Siebengebirge with the outstanding Drachenfels adjoin in pastel shades.

Stella looks in the distance, then , as if she could catch there an answer to her questions. "So what's up with your mysterious hints?" She turns to Mario.

"You're pretty impatient," he notes. "I told you it is a very complicated story. And before I start, you have to promise to not speak to anyone, not even the police. "

"Why not? It's the most natural thing in the world to go to the police immediately if you find out anything suspicious about a robbery. "

"Usually yes. But in this case it is different. You know I have a sister. Do you remember?"

"Yes, her name is Melanie. I remember her. Doesn't she live near Dresden, does she? "

"Correct. This is my sister , she is married to a car mechanic who works in a large workshop, along with other colleagues. And now it's about these two, Melanie and her husband Gregor. Oh and by the way is Melanie pregnant at the moment. "

"That's nothing special," says Stella. "But of course very gratifying and congratulations anyway!"

"Both of them are of course very happy," Mario continues, "but Melanie has problems in her pregnancy. She has to lie a lot and she 's not allowed to get upset. When she was lying on the couch the other day and nodded off a bit, her husband was talking quietly to a work colleague in the living room. She woke up and could understand a few chunks of the conversation while the two men thought that she was still asleep. "

"Aha, and then she heard that the colleague robbed the Green Vault, right?"

"No of course not! If it had been that easy! The two talked about an other colleague. Namely a , of a friend to the car , which is in itself nothing unusual. But they were talking about a car with a dark roof and a gold-colored body, just as the police described one of the getaway cars. And they also talked about the fact that the colleague and his friend are both very good at welding . You have to do that if you want to repair cars. "

"Ah yes, the bars of the window is indeed to have been welded. Now Melanie probably suspects that the colleague and his friend are the jewel thieves, right? "

"Yes, she suspects that immediately after this conversation, and in the evening she asked her husband, which she confided that she heard the cell. But he said to her that she must have misunderstand something. There was no question of that at all. And she should rather not talk to anyone about it, because the police assume that the criminals were very careful and planned in the robbery of this jewel and that they could not be trifled with. So if she utters careless suspicions to the police or anywhere else, it is very dangerous for her and the whole family. Because there were professionals at work, certainly a whole group of people who are not to be trifled with. "

"And what does that mean now? Does he want to solve the case himself or maybe even blackmail the perpetrators? Then you really have to go to the police. "

"Oh no! That would be far too dangerous. In this workshop are some sorts of rumors that are going in all directions, and my brother in law has to be very careful.. Especially because the boss is currently favoring the two suspects , and on another occasion he has threatened to throw my brother-in-law redundant if he does not behave in an absolutely friendly manner with them . There was also something that wasn't entirely kosher, and in which he covered the two suspects. "

Stella grimaces. "I don't really understand the whole thing. Can't Gregor find another job can he? And why is he afraid of these men? They certainly don't know that he heard something. "

"But! That is exactly what happened. The two suspects eventually discovered my brother-in-law and advised him not to draw the wrong conclusions from what he had heard. And they also threatened him that if he let anyone know anything that could give them a bad name, he would have to expect anything from them. And by "everything" they certainly didn't mean anything good. "

"That sounds very suspicious, and to me also criminal. Your brother-in-law just has to go to the police. "

Mario shook his head. "You really don't understand anything. They may be really criminals. And before the police can intervene, they'll do anything to Melanie or Gregor. It happens so quickly, the police cannot intervene that fast. "

"Doesn't he have a good opinion of the police does he? They will definetely find a solution , how to protect them. And besides, these criminals cannot prove who betrayed them. It could have been anyone. "

"Definitely not. I think one of the mechanics already has a criminal record, he probably doesn't like to see the police show up on him. Such people are always very sensitive. "

"Has your brother found out anything, for example where the loot is? Did they already bring the jewelry abroad? Dresden is not that far from the border. They must have changed the getaway car somewhere. "

" Yes, my sister suspects that too. We have already talked about it in more detail. There must have been several perpetrators, and everything was probably carefully planned beforehand. That's why it went so quickly and so smoothly. "

"But what am I supposed to do with the whole thing now? Why did you include me there? I don't know what tI should do now. And I also don't know how I can help you or your sister. "

"I didn't even get the idea myself," he apologizes. "It was my sister who made her own thoughts. On the one hand, she asked if she might be allowed to visit you if the whole thing was getting too hot for her. And on the other hand, she said that she also had an idea about the jewelry. But she didn't tell me anything about that personally. She just wanted to discuss that with you. I really don't know what it's about, although I've already given it some thought. In any case, I cannot imagine that she has any idea where the stolen jewelry is kept. I just think that as a resident of Dresden, she thinks this jewelry is just as great as you do. These old treasures are really precious, and I remember that you used to rave about this jewelry to me. "

"Yes, she's right. There are really so many treasures in Dresden, not just the historical buildings, the fantastic jewels, but also this exquisite and magical porcelain. I was always excited when I looked at it. Dresden is always worth a trip, and Melanie should be happy that she lives there. "

"So what is it now? Could you imagine talking to my sister, maybe on the phone first? But I definetely don't want to put you of risk. I want to buy you a special cell phone that you can only use while talking to my sister. Or would you prefer to write to her by email. She wants to change her cell phone all the time and go to a safe place to make calls so that no one can tap her. "

"But she is pretty clever when she wants to observe all such precautionary measures. Is she perhaps a detective? "

"No. So far she has not been active in this way. But now because of the inadvertently overheard conversation she startet to be careful. And if you are afraid, you think about some precautionary measures. "

"All right, then you can get me this cell phone and she can contact me. Is that all? Can I go home now? I would like to jog a little more. "

He gives her a long look. "Yes, if you want. That was what I absolutely had to tell you personally today. "

She looks at him confused. Is that all now? Doesn't he want to repeat his vows of love again, does he? Did he really just bring her here because of the jewel heist? She is almost disappointed that he doesn't talk about his feelings again.

"Fine, I'll go now. Just get in touch when you have the cell phone. You can tell Melanie that I agree. If she really wants to be away from Dresden for a few days, she can come to me. And I'll have an open ear for her worries. "

"Thank you, Stella. She will be grateful to you and so am I. See you soon!"

With an indefinable feeling in her stomach, the young woman turns away from him and makes her way back . She admits that she was secretly hoping that he would at least give her a quick kiss on the cheek. Is that his new tactic of, or did he just want to leave the decision to her?

It starts to rain gently. On her arrival at home, she first takes a shower and warms herself up again under the hot, spraying jet. Again and again her thoughts find her way back to Mario. Yes, that's probably what he intended. He wants to irritate her so that she thinks of him more often. But she doesn't want to do him the favor. There are enough other things that are interesting right now.

After the shower, she goes back to the texts and pictures for Wednesday evening and delves into them.

***

5th chapter

"What do you want to do now?" Asks Silvia after Stella has told her every detail about the meeting with Mario.

The young woman is nibbling on a pretzel stick.

"At the moment I can't do anything, I have to wait and see what the whole story is about. Mario and his sister just talkedon the phone, maybe there are some misunderstandings. But I'll find out, don't worry! "

"Aren't you afraid the whole thing could be dangerous if the whole thing is really true are you? It's all so mysterious. Everything is just suspicions, even the hint that you cannot go to the police does not sound particularly reassuring. Either the whole thing is extremely dangerous , or it's just a fantasy.

His sister may have hatched this plan with Mario so she can help bring you back together. I wouldn't believe everything blindly. "

"Well, it's really hard to believe that I can't go to the police with this whole thing. Because she is certainly very cautious and discreet in such cases. However, there are always blackmail stories in which the blackmailed do not dare to go to the police so that the danger does not become even worse. He really put me in two minds. And of course my feelings irritated, because he was totally objective at this meeting. "

"That is definitely just a trick", Silvia suspects. "Now he has first made contact with you. He can now officially meet you again, he made it. And he wants to give you the cell phone too, couldn't he send that to you by mail too? "

"It's safer personally than by mail," says Stella in defense. " And one meeting is enough for that, so I don't open my door for him for the long term."

"So you can definitely count on me," offers Silvia. "I will be as secretive as a grave and of course I won't tell Jens anything about it. And I hope you don't have to go to Dresden for that too. As long as you are here, at least you are still far from the gunshot, so I'm still a little reassured. Is there actually also a reward for the one who finds the culprit or even brings the jewelry back? "

"Certainly. And when we get a reward, we both take a trip to Venice. Do you like that? "

"Of curse. I've always been in love with all the winding alleys and the countless bridges and idyllic places. The whole atmosphere of the Serenissima is a pleasure for everyone with an artist's eye, and not just for them. This elderly lady wears her wrinkles with such elegance and indescribable charm like no other city. And you are not afraid now? "

Stella smiles. "Not yet. I still feel safe because I'm looking at the whole thing from a distance and so far none of the perpetrators knows that I intend to spy a little with Melanie. As long as I don't know anything, I don't have to be afraid. The fact is, however, that the robbers are definitely not squeamish, probably not unscrupulous, because they did it in such a short time period with such good nerves. "

"You don't really know whether they weren't really nervous and whether their hands were shaking while welding. But it must have been professionals, otherwise the whole thing would certainly not have worked. It was completely staged. "

"You surely have a good hiding place for the jewels. You don't just keep something like that in the fridge,"Stella muses.

Silvia is amused. " Why not? This is where the jewelry is the least noticeable , and it stays there well, in a cool temperature. "

"At the moment we can still laugh about it, hopefully we won't be drawn into this criminal case."

"I'm afraid , you started, Stella. If you want to stay out of it completely, you don't have to accept Mario's suggestion. Is it really that important is it ? Is there no one else his sister can visit? Can't he take care of her? "

"He only lives in a tiny room, there is really no room for Melanie. And as long as we stay here in Bonn, probably nothing can happen to us. Dresden is quite a long way from here, and I don't think that Mario's sister is being watched by anyone who drives her this far. I think you should not worry too much. And who knows? Maybe she would rather not leave her husband alone. Why should she want to travel here with a hard pregnancy? "

"Right, that's the question. She's probably lying in bed all day. How does she want to make the long journey and in which vehicle? It's all still pretty inconsistent and contradicting. I still don't trust Mario. Maybe he really just wants to slowly get back to you with it. I advise you to give yourself a few more thoughts about it before you finally agree with him. "

"Good, if you think so. I'm not sure what to think or what to do. "She changes the subject and tells her friend about the pictures for the preparation of the children's service. "I also don't know what came over me. It kind of moved me. It all reminded me of the past , of my own time at church service . I think that shaped me a lot. At that age I was very receptive to things that lay behind everything that was visible , and from then I have always had good experiences with praying. "

"If the children notice that you believe in what you convey to them, then it is not difficult for them to accept something from you. I can also remember the time when I went to the children's service. The fact that my memories were not so good was probably due to my parents, who made it my duty to go there regularly and of course every Sunday . That's why I never really felt like it. It always took me a while to get myself ready to go to church. It was probably easier for you then. "

Stella smiles. "It is really strange how quickly a person can be against something that is presented to him as a duty. I actually went there quite voluntarily, no one forced me. So I was very un biased and had great joy. Why do people actually have such aversions to their duties? "

"Yes, I experience that every day with the children in kindergarten. Everything they do voluntarily is much more fun for them. Nevertheless, we are not allowed to present everything that is compulsory as fun. That would not properly prepare the children for life. Indeed, they have to learn to do something that is less fun for them and that is made a duty to them. "

"It's a shame," Stella thinks. "Would not it be possible to represent nothing but mandatory, so it s just makes everything fun would it?"

Silvia laughs. "I haven't thought about that yet. But tonight I'm too tired for such philosophical thoughts. Jens is already calling me, I think he misses me. It's really nice in a partnership, but it also happens that Jens becomes a real burdock. Get me right, I love him, but now and then it almost looks as if he is jealous when the two of us are talking on the phone. "

Stella joins the friend's laughter. "There is no rose without thorns. I am now looking forward to Wednesday and hope that I have found my new hobby, until than or maybe even more. Maybe it really is something that gives my life a special meaning. "

"That is quite possible, Stella. I'm also glad that Jens and I both believe so firmly in God. I couldn't imagine being married to an atheist. It is the right partnership basis, because , once we trust and we find a way back to our harmony. Oh no, please don't take this personally. I really haven't alluded to this Mario business now. It's something completely different, something serious. I can really understand that you haven't forgiven him until today. "

Stella distracts from the topic and tells about Benno. "It's strange, almost a bit fateful, that I met him again during the storm pouring under the roof."

"That sounds really good. He seems like a nice person, just like you said about him. And I also think that he likes animals is a good sign. And what a coincidence that he lives so close to you. If you look out of the skylight, you might even wave to him. "

"Not a bad idea," says Stella with a smile and pours herself a cup of tea. "Have a nice evening with Jens and say hello from me. Tell him not to be angry, and certainly not to be jealous of me. After all, we've both known each other for many, many years. Those were the days at school! I am gonna go for a walk with Moni, and after that I am gonna get comfortable on the couch. "

The two say goodbye and agree to have a phone call on Wednesday evening because Silvia would like to see how Stella liked the preparation for the children's service.

Stella puts the cell phone aside, puts Moni on a leash and walks on Don-Bosco-Straße past the school where she was taught once in earlier years.

On the other side of the street, she sees a male figure and cannot believe her eyes. It's Benno, smiling towards her. Is it just a coincidence, or if did he know , that it's about that time again with the dog on the road?

He greets her and she looks at her with shining eyes. "How nice that we meet again. I thought that it would be good if I make friends with this nice little dog. It's definitely better if I go for a walk with a dog who knows me. I can at least imagine it that way. Or what about your little one? "

"That's a great idea. Moni is very trusting and friendly to the most peaple, I guess that's why I only know nice people. There are also people she doesn't like, with whom she withdraws or simply ignores them. "

"May I stroke you?"

"Of course, gladly. You certainly know your way around dogs, I don't have to explain anything to you. "

Benno slowly crouches down and carefully holds his hand in front of Moni's black nose so that she can smell his hand. The dog sniffs excitedly and briefly licks his fingers. Benno raises his hand cautious and petts the Poodle behind his ears in the curly hair.

"She's not a typical poodle at all. Most of them look a bit sophisticated. She just looks like a normal dog to me, not a decorative figure. Nor is her hair as flashy as many other poodles. Nice of course, and I like that. "

"That's exactly what I intended, I keep her like a normal dog. I don't want to go to any fashion show with her. During the education I also made sure that she was brought up quite normally, but did not have to endure a thousand different training sessions. "

"Should we take a few steps together? Would you like to let me have the leash for a few meters? "He suggests.

"Gladly. So Moni can get used to you holding her leach. I love the forest here, shall we take a few steps there? "

Benno nods. "It smells particularly good at this time of the day. And for Moni there is sure to be something to sniff. "

The two young people walk side by side with the small, lively dog through the mixed forest of the Kottenforst. They listen to the birds singing in the evening, the rustling of the leaves through which a gentle wind blows. While the sunlight is wandering deeper and deeper between the trees, Stella talks about her varied work at the hat maker. Benno listens carefully to her and expresses his interest with a few detailed questions.

Moni allows herself to be led without hesitation and shows no deviant, conspicuous behavior during the evening walk , he seems to accept Benno as an accompanying person.

As the insulation spreads between the trees , the two of them return and say good-bye in a good mood at Stella's front door. They say goodbye with a firm hug.

***

6th chapter

At the meantime Anton and Wolfgang lay next to Rothenburg in Upper Lausitz near the Polish border, a wooden plate over the deep hole they dug in the old barn. The well-stocked safe is well hidden deep down .

A few shovels of clay cover the wooden plate and are carefully trampled on by the two men .

"So, now the old junk above it again, " suggests Anton. "Everything is really safe for now. Nobody will find it here. "

Wolfgang grimaces. "I'm not that sure about that," he says skeptically. "We should have listened to Hugo . Since the Polish border is so close, he offered us that we could bring the stuff to his relatives. I still believe that that would have been better. "

"Nonsense. The police will surely think that the things were brought from Dresden to Poland immediately. And nobody would think that the jewelry is so close to Dresden. No one gusses thatnobody. You always have to go the unlikely paths and not the ones that you can always think of immediately. I'm much more worried about Gregor in the garage. I'm not sure if we can keep this going. Of course I threatened him that something would happen if he didn't hold up. But he's already such a chatterbox , and that's definitely dangerous. "

"But he also acted really dumb. How can he talk to you at home about it while his wife is on the couch and listens to everything. "

"He has adapted really damn stupid," says Anton, shaking the long tangled hair. " Even if he pretended to be a colleague, his wife could track him down. You could have come up with the idea only because he doesn't have an alibi for the time of the robbery. "

Wolfgang shakes his head vigorously. "No, I don't think she believes that her husband does something like this. And he works so many times until midnight. Surely she will not be able to imagine that he is involved in it. But she may now inquire intensively about these alleged colleagues. And that's enough to somehow track us down. We have to think about something. "

Anton thinks about it. "Well, the simplest thing would be for him to talk about these two alleged colleagues again as if by chance. And then he just has to announce that he was wrong about the suspicions. How does he even think of telling such nonsense. "

"It happened purely by chance. We talked about overmoulding the car. Then Gregor heard some noise from his wife and realized that she was lying on the couch nearby and must have woken up. And then he made up the story with his colleagues, in case she heard anything from the previous conversation. "

" Gregor is such an Idiot", says Anton. "We should have taken other accomplices. In any case, someone with a bigger brain. "

"Good that Gregor is out of our deal, he only has to get his wage. Did Ivan contacted you again? What does he think of all the next steps? "

Anton opens a bottle of beer. " He actually tried to push the price down. And so I'm not sure if we shouldn't find another lover and buyer for all the jewelry who pays more than this rich Russian multimillionaire. There are sure enough collectors all over the world. Furthermore, I'm not that sure anymore if Ivan reveals us afterwards. After all, we don't know his real name or address. "

Wolfgang thinks about it. "It may well be that Ivan deliberately allows so much time to pass so that afterwards we can sell him the stuff cheaper, because we are on fire here and because we want to get the money as quickly as possible."

"After all, the jewelry is safe here now. The previous hiding place didn't suit me. Let's get out of here, not that anyone else finds us here . Will you be able to park the motorcycle again unnoticed at your fathers house in the barn? "

Wolfgang takes a long swig from the bottle. "Of course. He doesn't even know that this motorcycle still exists. He's usually already demented. Come on, everything is fine and safe here now. "

The two push the motorcycle out of the barn where they had hidden it during their stay and go outside. A rough wind greets them. They quickly put on their helmets and swing on the two-wheeler. They drive back to Dresden via Görlitz and Bautzen.

Wolfgang stops at the northern edge of Dresden - Neustadt and lets his buddy dismount. They give each other a quick wave, then part. While Anton rushes through the northern part of the city, his friend continues in the direction of Jena.

Both men think again about Gregor, and especially about his carelessness to have shared something about the car at home. Anton makes a decision and goes to Gregor's local pub. It's an old, somewhat dingy pub where several men sit at the counter in the twilight and enjoy the beer after work.

A bearded man is talking to Luise, the owner. Anton speaks to him from the side. "Hey, Gregor! Work is already done for today? "

The addressed turns around suddenly. "What do you want here? Is there anything special? "

"Not that I know," says Anton dizzy. "How is your wife? Is she still pregnant? "

"Yes. Why?"

"Two beers!" Anton orders from Luise. " Your wife is fine? Then we hope it will stay that way. You have to be very nice to her. Then she will be fine too. "

"Of course", Gregor looks at him in astonishment, "because I'm always very nice to her. I love my wife and I want her to be well. That's very clear "

Anton throws him a threatening look. "Then if I were you I would do everything I can to keep it that way . Hopefully you won't upset the woman with adventurous stories, will you ? "

"Of course not. Maybe I'll send her on vacation for a few days so that she can relax a bit. She still has a brother in the Rhineland who invited her. "

"A good idea," praises Anton. "I think we got along. But remember, I'm always around and take good care of yourself so that nothing happens to you either. "

He throws a banknote on the counter and leaves the restaurant with a brief greeting.

Gregor remains brooding. He's not comfortable with the whole thing because Anton doesn't seem to trust him. He has to think about something so that in future he is no longer under suspicion of telling his wife something . And now he can't think of anything else at the moment, he orders another beer.

***

7 . chapter

It's Wednesday evening. The windows of most apartment' s in the row houses are dark. The moon shines through the kitchen window while Stella is on the phone with her friend. "I was eagerly waiting for your call," confesses Silvia . "Jens has been sleeping for a while. How was the preparation of the children's service? "

"It was really nice, and I think if I have just as much fun with the children on Sunday, then I've really found a meaningful pastime for myself. The men and women who are also active are very nice. And the pastor would not mind using my drawings to decorate stories with pictures. He said, however, that it could be a lot of work for me in the long run if I wanted to paint a series of pictures for every Sunday. Some really lived the idea. A nice young man, whose daughter also attends the children's church service, would also like to enrich his stories with pictures in the future. "

Silvia is happy with her friend. "That are great news. Did you also have to explain how you imagine the interpretation of this story? "

"Yes , it is important to this pastor that we transfer the story into today's everyday life of the children so that they feel addressed . For now , he assigned me the group of five to six year olds, so I should try it at the beginning. There are about six to eight children who will probably visit my group next Sunday . I'm really excited. You can certainly imagine that. "

"I'm also very curious what you have to tell me then. And what about Benno and Mario now? Is there anything new? "

Stella takes a sip of tea from the delicate porcelain cup. " The nice dog lover now goes for a walk with Moni and me every evening. Yesterday we were up to Waldau, and all three of us had a lot of fun. We have found that we both quite like to travel. But most of all, I think, he loves a cozy home. He told me that he's been married before but that his ex-wife is causing so many difficulties. He also has a young son, but his wife has influenced him so much that he has little desire to see his father. Those seem some mothers outstanding to, I think , it should be punished. "

"I have also heard from such cases that the mothers tell the children terrible stories about the fathers and manipulate them completely. It is very mean. Then he will certainly suffer from it. "

"Yes, but he tries to look at it objectively, and he hopes that his son will understand everything later. He wants a family with as many children as possible, but at the moment he's still in the process of healing the wounds of his past marriage. "

"Wouldn't that be something for you, Stella?"

"Oh, I'm not exactly keen on a new partnership either. A nice friendship is perfect at the moment. Mario got in touch again and asked when I could take his sister Melanie in for a few days. She had wanted the whole time, but now even her husband, Gregor, suggested that she take her to Bonn by mobile home. "

"With the mobile home? Why?"

"Everything is very convenient in a mobile home. You have a very soft armchair on the passenger side, even with footrests. Gregor inherited this expensive motorhome from his late father, a true luxury motorhome. Melanie always wants to sell it because they don' t have that much money and still need a lot for the future. But Gregor doesn't want to sell it because it reminds him of his father and that's why he is attached to it. "

" Well what! And when will Mario's sister be with you then? "

"From tomorrow evening. I'm really excited about that, after all, I haven't seen her for a while. I used to get on well with her, though, and I don't see why that shouldn't be the case now. But I'm a little worried about her pregnancy. After all, I'm working half a day and then she's alone. "

"Well, I think she's even more alone at home. When her husband works so much overtime in the workshop, he'll definitely not come home until night. You're only gone for a few hours in the morning, she 'll be able to cover that. "

"Yes, and I've already spoken to the boss that I might be able to take a job or two home with me . Depending on how skillfully Melanie is doing, she can even help me a little, then she won't get so bored. "

"Not a bad idea, Stella. And I don't think you need to worry about anything else either , the clinic is right around the corner from here. She can almost walk there if there is anything. "

"Yes, I thought so too. And yet I'm not entirely satisfied with the whole thing. You know, when a young couple is expecting a child, the man is also happy to be very close to his wife. Did they really quarrel because of this stupid misunderstanding and the suspicious conversation? "

"I think if you live in Dresden you can get upset when this valuable and beautiful jewelry is so brutally stolen. Presumably the thieves not only brutal criminals, but also have no relation to this magnificent city, its our history and its art treasures. You have to have at least a lot of respect for that. You have already told me a lot about your relatives from Dresden. And every time I hear from your stories how deeply you are rooted in the city. Every time you talk about Dresden, you start to rave about it. "

Stella smiles . "Yes, that's the way it is . And that's why I'm personally really mad at the art thieves. I have my worst fears when I imagine that they separate the stones from the gold and simply melt the gold down. That would be a terrible sacrilege! "

"Hopefully the thieves aren't that mean and so ignorant. After all, these individual pieces of jewelery have a much higher value than artistic jewels if they remain untouched. "

Stella sighs. "I hope the whole case will be cleared up soon. After all, we have a hard-working police force, and there is likely to be a high reward for those who can provide clues. I'm curious whether Melanie can tell me anything more specific. In any case, she will have it quieter here with me. "

"I took a few days off because Jens and I want to renovate the apartment. But I'm just wondering whether I can just drop by your apartment every morning to see how your guest is doing. What do you think about that?"

"If you want to take the trouble, that's a great idea, Silvia. I feel a little more comfortable with this thought so Melanie don't has to spend the morning here alone. Do you think you can do it despite the renovation work? "

" Sure. After all, you have to take breaks when renovating. And there is also work determines where   Jens did not want me to be there. Sometimes he is so absorbed in his work that he does not notice anything around him. Then maybe I get in his way from time to time. I will discuss everything with him. And how do you do that on Sunday with the children's church service? "

"If Melanie doesn't have to stay in bed all the time, we will drive to the church by car. I can imagine that it won't hurt her to sit there for an hour if we can find a comfortable chair. "

"Oh yes. Then everything has been thought of, but if you still need any help, you can contact me, Stella! "

"Thank you! Incidentally, Mario can also give himself a few thoughts , and he should visit his sister here now and then. I expect that from him. "

Now Silvia sighs. "He'll probably be too happy to do that. I still think he's just using it as an excuse to get closer to you again. Just be careful not to let him ingratiate yourself with you again! "

"I will do everything I can to resist his charm, " promises Stella.

The two women say goodbye to each other.

Moni comes jumping over and demands her every evening petting.

When Stella lies in bed a little later and wants to relax, a series of thoughts go through her head. Is it really good to allow contact with Mario again? When they met again, she clearly felt that she still had feelings for him, significantly more than she would like. This is surely due to the fact that the past time with him was so indescribably beautiful . She remembers the short vacation trip with him to the Dolomites. She didn't like his driving style, he drove way too fast, like the kind of man who always likes to play racing. But when they then walked over the mountain meadows, hand in hand, she had the feeling that nothing stood between them and that nothing could ever separate them. She had felt that he enjoyed nature as much as she does. They had breathed deeply the fresh mountain air, listened to the lonely calls of the birds, stood still in front of the gigantic mountains, one of the great wonders of nature. They had enjoyed the bees above the mountain flowers, listened to the rushing of the torrents, stood speechless in front of the thundering waterfalls and felt the sun on their skin together.

Yes, he is a person of the open senses, summarizes these thoughts about him, this harmony is not a matter of course for a couple. He had also been sensual to the touch, how he had enjoyed her caresses, and she had been able to feel it herself , this gentle vibration on the skin, the pulsation of the blood in a heartbeat! The first night full of tenderness and restrained passion was also unforgettable. When he first kissed the palm of her hand, little sparks glowed in his eyes and he promised her a festival of the seven delicacies like a Chinese meal . He meant his kisses in all variations, light and gentle like those of butterflies, intimate and intense like scented roses, jasmine and honey wine, and finally passionate like an erupting volcano. In fact , she had felt all these feelings with him , and a finale in which she believed that the earth was shaking and blazing in flames.

That night with him was deeply engraved in her memory back then. She had cherished this memory like a precious piece of jewelry, tightly locked in the jewelry box of the past , deep in her memory .

For her birthday he had surprised her with a large bouquet of red roses, baked her a cake himself and took her out to dance in the evening because she loved dancing with him so much . That was in a small dance hall in Bonn. In the dim light she had confided in his arms, let him lead her with her eyes closed. In every rhythm her steps harmonized like magical vibrations , she turned to him devotedly when they came together to the sounds of the music as in a fairytale symbiosis of fairy beings .

An unforgettable birthday!

So many unforgettable days when she was happy with him. Didn't you always have to keep such beautiful memories clearly in mind as beautiful days instead of drying them out or freezing them do you? No, it had hurt too much to think about it so far.

She feels within herself. Does it still hurt that much doesn't it? It does not hurt so much, she is relieved and the letters of love had actually contributed as a balm to heal the wound. So she has to be extra careful now so that she doesn't fall in love with him again. But she clearly feels that there something between them. That's dangerous.

How did Silvia say to her the other day? "The tingling in love grows with the hopelessness."

Stella looked at her blankly. "What do you mean by that?"

Silvia had smiled mysteriously. "Some people just love the adventurous thing about love. Forbidden love is the hit. And I personally also believe that those who have an unpredictable factor are particularly prickly. On the other hand , the boring partnerships probably last the longest. "

"How reassuring," Stella had commented. "Then it's best to marry your good friend."

"Yes, for example," Silvia had added.

Stella sighs and sees the moonlight through the window. The unpredictability factor probably exists in Mario and me, the young woman suspects . " But today I won't be able to clarify this question. "

***

8th Chapter

Melanie makes herself comfortable in the armchair. "I don't even know how to thank you, Stella ?! You're really helping me a lot by taking me in here for a few days. I didn't feel so comfortable at home alone anymore. "

Stella hands her a cup of steaming tea. "You really don't have to thank me . It doesn't bother me at all . Why do I have this guest room here in this pretty little apartment ?! And it really is time for someone to initiate it. What was it most that bothered you at home? The fact that you were always alone for so many hours and Gregor couldn't help you? Or are you afraid of the story with the jewels. "

Melanie stirs the teacup. "To be honest, it was very uncomfortable all day alone without someone, but the feeling that there are people in Gregor's company who are involved in the crime scene makes me even more afraid. Although my husband has assured me that it was a misunderstanding, I am quite sure that I heard correctly and that he spoke about a colleague. "

"You were asleep, couldn't you have misunderstood something while you were half asleep?"

"I've been puzzling over this all the time . At least Gregor wanted to convince me that. But so far I have always been able to rely on my good ears for sure . "

"And what does your husband say about that?"

"He forbade me to talk about it. He says his boss would kick him out otherwise. I can't risk that. "

Stella frowns. "I can't quite understand that. Does the boss hold his hand in the fire for all his employees? There can be a black sheep among them everywhere. And the boss should only be happy if his company is free from the suspicion that one of his employees is a criminal. So, in terms of logic, none of this fits together at all. "

"I think so too. But Gregor is just happy that I'm gone now and can't go any further. "

Stella looks carefully at Melanie. "Do you actually love your husband?"

"Oh! How do you come to that in that context? I can't understand that at all now. You mean because he's glad I'm gone now? "

"Oh no. I think he's just happy that you're well looked after now because otherwise he might have to worry about you all the time while he works. And then he is probably really uncomfortable at the moment when you ask him about this topic of jewel theft. No, my question was very general now. But maybe it is too private for you. "

" No, that's not too private for me. We knoe each other for a long time now. But what does love mean? Of course, at some point I promised myself something different from being together. I was hoping we'd spend more time together, and now he's in the workshop all day and into the night. But of course I should be happy about it, because he earns more, and a small family definitely needs a lot of money. "

"Yes, everyday life often puts a strain on the feelings of being in love, I think so too. But how about love, could you imagine a life without him? "

"I haven't tried that yet. So it's all pretty routine with us. A short breakfast with few words in the morning. A quick kiss at midnight. He usually also works on Saturdays, and on Sundays he is happy when he can sleep in and relax in front of the television. Isn't that the case in many marriages? "

"That may be, I don't know. But imagine if you had to be without him, what would you be missing then? "

Melanie thinks about it. "I would probably find the bed next to me empty and also the armchair in front of the TV on Sunday. As I said, it's all routine. And then a piece of this routine would be missing. But that's not important at all now. After all , we're having a baby that I'm really looking forward to. We become parents and Gregor becomes a father. It's a gift and it will certainly weld us together. "

Stella pours tea into the dainty cups again. "Oh no. You're kidding. I was married once too, to Niels. But we have grown apart completely in a very short time. Fortunately, we had no children at the time, and when we discovered that we had to part in order not to harm each other, we made sure that we no longer have a baby. We were both glad that we were spared the trouble of comforting a separated child and raising it with difficulties. "

"You were probably right about that. I 'm really focused on the baby, and I look forward to it too. I want to confess something to you too. I often look for the feelings I had about Gregor at the beginning. But I thought that it is how it is with all marriages. Then the children become important and you just have to be careful not to argue like that. Maybe I just imagined I was in love at the beginning, it's so hard to get behind your own feelings. But little Katharina, that's what we want to call our baby, she's all I have now. "

Stella smiles and takes Melanie in her arms. "I'm sorry for asking you so directly. It really matters now that you look forward to the baby. How many days are now until the expected date? "

"Exactly a fortnight and my doctor told me it could come a little earlier. I don't even think about it if the little one wants to come today or tomorrow. I've already called a midwife here from Dresden who wants to come by tomorrow. And the clinic is right around the corner. "

"Wouldn't you miss Gregor at birth? Doesn't he want to be there?

"No, it still seems to be of the very old-fashioned kind. He thinks he will pass out watching a birth. And he doesn't want me to do that. One is just not another. That's why I'm happy to be here. "

"I actually thought that Mario would come to greet you here today too. After all, you haven't seen each other in a long time. Have you spoken to him yet? "

"Yes I have. But he has such a cold that he doesn't want to come so he don't want to infect me. It could also be a virus or a flu. "

"It makes sense that he doesn't visit you then . But how is he? Does he have a fever? Does he need help? "

"He is doing quite well and he thinks he can manage on his own. But we will of course still be on the phone, and he will certainly also write me one or two short messages. But tell me what kind

of wonderful plants do you have on your balcony?
"

Stella smiles. "The balcony is my little garden . On the left side you can see all my kitchen herbs that bloom and grow, and some of them smell very aromatic. Mint, for example, or sage, lemon balm and lavender. And the rest, these are all my flower children in pots and as small ornamental shrubs. They all took the move here very well. "

"Wonderful, I also love the flowers and nature. I'm sure you're going to go for a walk with Moni. Today I'm still a little too tired from the long journey, but tomorrow I would like to take you for a walk. I heard that the neighboring Kottenforst is such a beautiful forest. Mario always raved about that to me. "

Stella looks at the clock. "You're right. This is the time for Moni's evening stroll. Can I leave you alone for so long? "

"Of curse. Today you don't even need an umbrella, unlike the last few days. Have fun. During that time, I'll talk to Mario on the phone. Until Gregor gets back home in Dresden, that will definitely take until midnight. That's a lot of kilometers between Bonn and Dresden. "

"Do you need anything else, Melanie? Are you still hungry or hungry or want something sweet? "

The young woman shakes her head. "Oh no! Dinner was so plentiful, and then there was this sweet little dessert. I haven't eaten that much for a long time because it just doesn't taste that good to me alone. "

"Well! Then I'll be gone for half an hour, but I'll take the cell phone with me. You can call me anytime."

"Don't make yourself crazy! I'm in good hands here in your pretty little apartment. And Katharina likes it here too. I notice that because she moves so lively. "

Stella puts the dog on a leash and hurries out of the apartment, hops down the stairs and looks around outside. Will Benno be waiting?

Indeed, he is at the back of the garden fence and looks expectantly in their direction. The young woman rushes over to him. "I am sorry that I am late today and that you have been waiting for us . I just messed up with Melanie. But she is fine and now I can calmly leave her alone for a few minutes. "

Benno gives her a friendly look. "Do not worry! The fresh air here was good for me. The main thing is that your guest is doing well after the long journey. And right now the blackbirds are singing particularly well. "

From here you can hear the Apfelallee Abendlied and a blackbird. Benno bends over and pats Moni, who happily licks his hand.

After an extensive welcoming ceremony the young man grabs the leash and leads the dog in the little side streets to the forest road. Stella adapts to his step and looks around the treetops.

"Now the leaves are almost fully grown. What a couple of rainy days did in such a short time. It is bursting with fresh green here. And everything looks like it has been washed clean . When I usually go a long way here , I often get the best ideas. "

"Should I leave you alone?" He jokes.

"But no. Today I don't need any new ideas. I took the first step when I decided to become a child worship service helper. And now I'm just curious to see how I'll do on Sunday. I hope the children will accept me. "

"Why shouldn't they? You exude a very natural authority, in the best sense of the word. And since you are so looking forward to it, I assume that it is really important to you to convey the words from the Bible. "

"Exactly. It really got me. I know how much faith has always carried me through life, through all difficulties. When people have disappointed me, God's Word has always rebuilt me, given me consolation, not let me despair until I found my way out of the bad times. It's actually like a lifeline or a floating island that you can float on in times of need. And then you also know that you will always be carried well, always protected. That's what happened to me at least, and you also know, everything has a sense. "

At that moment, Stella's cell phone answers.

The young woman carefully holds the phone to her ear. She hears Melanie 's voice that sounds excited: "Please come home. I think it's starting. "

***

9th chapter

Stella cradles the baby in her arms and looks at Melanie with shining eyes. "I congratulate you on this sweet person. Katharina is so beautiful! It is always a miracle when a child is born. "

Melanie is beaming. "I also think she's the cutest baby in the whole world. But I'm even more happy that she is completely healthy and that I got through the birth so quickly. I never thought it would be so fast. "

Benno is also happy. "The sisters all took me for the father. Your husband has to be proud when you give him such a beautiful daughter. Have you been able to reach him so far? "

"No, the battery on his cellphone is probably dead and he forgot to charge it. He's certainly still on the way. But when he arrives at home, he will definitely call me at home from the landline, "says Melanie.

"We had been thinking, Benno and I, if we can look for Gregor with a Reiseruf, but then we decided , to send him messages and to speak on his answering machine . Doesn't he have a charging cable for his mobile phone in the motorhome ? "Asks Stella.

"Yes , he already has. But although he is always such a neat and accurate person at work, at home and in the mobile home he is always looking for his belongings. So I'm not assuming that he'll recharge his cell phone on the go. If I assess it correctly, it thunders through to Dresden and then drives straight back to the workshop. I know him quite well now. "

Little Katharina makes herself noticeable, she cries a little in a soft, light voice. Melanie takes her tenderly in her arms. "Everything is fine with her, but she will be examined very thoroughly again in a moment. The doctor has already told me. It's just a precaution, and I'm glad they are so thorough here. "

"I think we'll leave you alone for a bit," says Benno. "Even if it was a very quick birth, it was definitely exhausting, and it's time you recovered a little."

"I think that's a good idea, too," says Stella. "A little sleep will do you good now. And probably us too. It's about midnight, Moni will be waiting impatiently. We'll visit you again tomorrow, I promise. "

"I would like to come to your home tomorrow," Melanie ponders. "But of course I don't want to cause you too much trouble. I prefer to stay in the clinic until I'm kicked out. Do you agree? "

Stella waves goodbye to the young mother . "Do what is best for you. And I'll send Mario another

voice message right away. But he wanted to know ,
if after examining all is well. But he doesn't want
to show up because of his cold. "

"I think that's very good," Melanie praises her
brother. "He really has a lot of responsibility. I
have a great brother. I'm not just saying that
because I want to put it in a good light with you .
He has always taken good care of me, even when I
was a little girl. I'll tell you a lot of nice stories
when I get the chance, Stella. "

"Yes, I believe you, and I'm looking forward to it.
I'm looking forward to the time you are staying
here with me in Bonn, and I'm also looking
forward to sweet little Katharina. But now it's time
for all of us to sleep. Good night darling!"

Benno and Stella say goodbye to the young mother
and smile once more at the little, newborn girl with
amorous looks.

The young man is whispering in the hallway. "She is a really cute little girl. But all little babies are cute . When I see a little one like that, I wish I had a child again. This Gregor doesn't seem to be very interested in his daughter . Otherwise he wouldn't have brought his wife here so shortly before the birth . Or how do you think about it? "

"Yes, that also seems very strange to me. Most men would have acted differently. I am curious to see how he will react when he receives the news that he has become a father. At some point , Benno , he'll probably listen to the phone and read his short messages . "

" And every other father would then turn around and come back to Bonn."

" Exactly. But we have to wait. But I just wanted to thank you for helping me so much with all of this now. You sacrificed the whole evening for Melanie and me and only had stress. First you took us to the clinic, then you drove back, took care of Moni again and got the things Melanie had forgotten. And now you've been here the whole time, patiently playing the surrogate father. No wonder the doctors and nurses thought you were the child's father. "

Benno grins. "I even liked it, I honestly have to admit that. Who does n't immediately take such a little baby into their heart ?! And Melanie is really a very nice woman. How is Mario her brother? And why does she want to tell you so many stories about him so badly? Is there a specific reason for that?"

The two step out of the clinic premises. The street lights only dimly light up the sidewalk. "You took such good care of Melanie and helped me like a true friend. You also deserve that I tell you the truth. Mario was once my great love. Back then it hit us like lightning, and it was very beautiful for a while, too beautiful probably. We wanted to get married , and I had already bought the wedding dress. That sounds like a bad movie now. But it really was. Shortly before the wedding, Mario allowed himself to be seduced by a spirited Mexican. He regretted it pretty quickly, at least that's what he said to me. He apologized and said that everything would be fine again. But I was hurt far too deeply and broke up with him. At first I left it open to see what my feelings about it say. But then I felt that since I 've lost confidence in him and the wound is simply too deep. Then I made him understand that it was over and that there was no point in waiting. Just a few days ago he got in touch and reminded himself again. First he gave me flowers, and then came this Melanie thing. I still do not know whether this idea to visit me himself came from Melanie or whether Mario had

this idea. I don't know, but I will probably find out.
"

"That sounds really strange," says Benno. " If I were you, I would be suspicious too. And what reasons did Melanie give you why she wanted to come here so badly? "

Stella sighs. "One reason was, of course, because Gregor is in the workshop and works all day and into the night. That was of course very difficult for the mother-to-be in every respect. But Melanie also has a very uncomfortable feeling at the moment because she fears that her husband might know something about the jewel robbery in Dresden. "

Benno is amazed and looks at the young woman with wide eyes. "Then she has to go to the police if she has seen and heard any suspicions or something."

"This is not so easy. Her husband and a colleague were talking while they believed she was sleeping on the sofa. They were talking about a car that had been sprayed around in the workshop and had been worked on by colleagues. And this car corresponded exactly to the very peculiar and rare car that the perpetrators escaped in. When Melanie spoke to Gregor about it, he talked himself out very threadbare. He spoke of a misunderstanding and that she must have misheard. It would not have been about her workshop , and he would have to be very careful, otherwise he would get in great trouble with the boss and his colleagues. Yes, he must have even voiced her fear that if he raised any suspicions, he might lose his job . So all around everything is pretty unclear. Because either he noticed something in the workshop and is afraid, or she misunderstood him, but then he shouldn't have to be afraid of his boss and being fired. Then I talked to Melanie about it again. But she says she is not entirely sure either , because in the last months of pregnancy she was very busy with herself and, of course, with thoughts about the child. It is theoretically also possible that she was mistaken. "

"Well, as far as I know, the jewels consuming not yet been clarified , I have only read once on the Internet that anyone has tried , the jewelry to sell, and another has tried to buy the jewelry. One would just have to look carefully and covertly into this company. A detective could do that, he could perhaps infiltrate himself as an office worker. "

"They probably don't need any new office workers there at the moment. Then perhaps mechanic, who is also a detective. But someone like that is definitely rare and will not be easy to find. "

"You are absolutely right. Then you would have to get the list of all employees. These individuals should monitor just privately let by a detective. But something like that is also an expensive affair. "

"I don't know Gregor. Something just occurred to me. "

"You don't know Gregor? But he brought Melanie here today. He must have carried up her suitcase and greeted you! "

"No! He didn't. He's a real coward. He wanted to go back immediately. He just called up in the hallway that his wife had arrived and another goodbye. Then he turned around and drove again. And then I quickly ran downstairs and brought Melanie and her suitcase to my apartment. "

"So I do not really understand that. What kind of impolite and insensitive person is that! But I don't understand what you mean by that now. What does that mean, you don't know Gregor? "

"Well, you know, it just occurred to me that I could smuggle me into the workshop myself , provided they need a new cleaning lady."

Benno laughs uproariously. "You want to go to Dresden, kick out the cleaning lady from the car company and apply yourself just to examine the car mechanics there a little closer?"

"Well, you have it perhaps not necessarily throw. You could poach them and lure them away, there are certainly different ways and meanings. At least it is worth considering. "

"I suggest you sleep one night before you make any further plans. After all, you are tired now after this exciting day , and we will be close to midnight or maybe already over. I'll take you to the door of your apartment first, and be not as rude as this Gregor. I want to be sure in any case, that you come home safely. "

"Thank you, Benno. Now you've hit your head half the night .Tomorrow morning you will be determined on the work and very tired to be. I'm sorry for you, and thank you for everything because you helped me and Melanie. "

"I was happy to do that, and I am always there for you again, if there is anything." He accompanies her up the stairs to the apartment door.

When they reach the top , he takes them again briefly in his arms. "And now you have to rest first. The day was long enough for you . How about Moni? Should I take her for another walk quickly? I wouldn't be happy if you were walking the streets alone in the dark. "

She unlocks the door, both of them greet the dog, with its friendly tail wagging, who is dancing around them .

"Maybe a very short walk, I'm grateful to you." She leashes Moni. "Here you have your loyal and grateful friend."

While he is running down the stairs with the animal, she thinks about Benno. What a good friend he is! He's so caring, thinks of everything. A smile crossed her face. What a happy woman I am, I was just able to experience how a child was born, I have a friend who is good to me and an ex-boyfriend who claims to love me. I have a job that I enjoy and am looking forward to a new job with children. Not everyone lives so well. Looking satisfied at the bouquet of roses, she sends a small prayer of thanks to heaven.

***

10. Chapter

The raindrops throw themselves at the windshield, the windshield wiper eagerly tries to clear the view of the oncoming headlights.

"Drive a little faster!" Wolfgang urges the man who is driving the car next to him.

"You are probably crazy," grumbles Gregor. "It's pitch black and it's raining twine. Do you think I want to kill myself? "

"If you don't drive so lame, the police or maybe Anton will kill you later because you will spoil everything. We are still a long way from the Polish border. "

Gregor lights a cigarette. "Damn it! It's your fault now. I said right away, take the car abroad immediately. It was injected around, nobody would have recognized it that quickly. "

"You have no idea about that. In the first few days they did a lot of checks , so this car would certainly have attracted attention . It was in good hands with Anton in the garage, nobody discovered it. The old garage had once rented his late aunt. Anton just kept paying the rent because he always had a good use for this garage. "

"Did he hide stolen cars in there?" Gregor blows a thick stream of smoke into the air. "I don't want anything to do with that."

Wolfgang grins. "You're right in the middle of it. Afterwards you cannot say that you have never seen the car. You injected the car by yourself, and somewhere there is still a trace of you, Anton will take care of that. "

"Oh, leave me alone with your illegal stuff! So far I haven't seen a cent for my work either. I am now driving around here in the countryside and should have been on my way to Bonn long ago. After all, I had a daughter a few hours ago and my wife will certainly expect me to come to her right away. "

"Don't be so hypocritical! Everyone but your wife knows that you had something with the boss's daughter. Nadja was always really keen on you. "

"That wasn't serious. And I also told her that it couldn't go on like this. If my wife finds out and she gets a divorce, then I have to sell the motorhome and give her half of the money. You don't know what the mobile home is worth ?! "

"No I do not know. But a lawyer is sure to find a way, they can twist everything until you're right. "

"Do you have a clue! The motorhome is well worth its 60,000 euros. It's kind of a life insurance policy for me. I'm also attached to the heirloom . "

Wolfgang snorts contemptuously. "The boss's daughter is a good match too, and she's still pretty hot for you. She also suits you a lot better, and you don't have to shut up in front of her. She knows everything. Hugo told her everything. "

Gregor throws the cigarette out the window. "Damn it, no. I finally want to get out of this milieu. Melanie is a decent woman who never suspected or knew anything about my astray. And so far it wasn't anything that interested the police. That you involved me in this injection molding plant in jewels was quite unfair. I wanted to lead a decent life now when the child is around. "

Wolfgang laughs out loud. "You do not believe it yourself. You have never been clean and you won't be. And you won't be able to get away from Nadja either, you can take poison on that. Besides, I don't even know why you're so upset. Tomorrow is also a day. Tomorrow you can also go to Bonn. After all, your wife cannot ask you to turn around immediately and drive this long distance back to Bonn from Dresden . You can tell her that it took you a few hours of sleep. She has to understand that. "

"If I at least had that! Instead of sleeping I am driving with this treacherous getaway car to Poland. "

"What do you want, Gregor. The license plates are new, the car is painted differently, it even has different lights, what more could you want? And if you drove a little faster, we would have crossed the border long ago. "

"When I get my money? I'm pretty dry right now, Wolfgang. I'm not putting myself in danger for nothing. "

"You're still getting your share! After all, we can't possibly sell the jewelry again just like that. We don't get anything and on top of that we go to prison. "

"If the jewelry is somewhere, it won't get any better. Do you even have a good hiding place? "

"Of course! And we have already changed it several times. You and Hugo don't know where things are at the moment. And that's good."

"Hugo got involved with that? He's the boss! ""He's only the boss in the workshop. Anton is the boss and he decides where to go. It's a very old thing, from the dark past. "

"What? Did the boss do anything criminal too? And he was stupid enough to tell Anton about it? "

"That was one of Hugo's youthful sin. Accurate I do not know anything else, only , that 's the boss still get into trouble when the device to the public. And that is indeed a very beautiful powerful male when you contrast you the tight Anton look at who is already something else. He won a lot of prices in boxing, and he is not squeamish. "

"I know that. He also threatened me that I should just keep my mouth shut. But of course I'm not that stupid and tell someone something about what I know. And I was able to calm my wife down quickly. Besides, she says nothing more. But I'll have to speak to Anton one more time. At least he had promised me an advance payment, and I haven't seen anything of it yet."

"Comfort yourself, I haven't seen a penny either. We just have to wait . You need patience with something like that, after all, it's not a completely normal theft. But it's also worth it afterwards. How much did Anton promise you? "

"I'm supposed to get a total of 100,000, and he wanted to give me an advance of 10,000 euros straight away, but I'm still waiting for that to this day."

"You'd better be patient, Gregor. You can't joke with Anton. He'll give you the money when the time comes. You didn't do that much in the whole matter. You are well served with your share of 100,000 euros . "

"I see it very differently. All this jewelry has an inestimable value of several million euros. I'm actually much more entitled to that. "He lights another cigarette.

"Don't smoke so much, Gregor! Look, the limit is already back there! You're talking about several million, what nonsense, Anton doesn't get that much for it. After all, you can't just sell it to the public that easily. You always have to compromise on the hand. And now let's see what's going on here at the border. Drive very slowly. At this time everything should be fine here. "

***

11th chapter

Melanie opens the door for Stella. "I actually slept one more time while you were at the children's service. I should be ashamed at this time of the day. But Katharina just slept so well, it was so tempting to close my eyes again. "

"That's good!" Says Stella. "Finally, cause you hadn't much sleep tonight. You have a lot to catch up on. I will now quickly bake a cake so that we can offer our guests something. "

"You do not have to. Benno called and said that he gets a cake at the café. And Mario got in touch too, because he's coming a few minutes later. His father still needs him on the mini golf course. "

Little Katharina answers, Melanie carefully takes her out of the basket and places her on her breast. Stella begins to prepare the table for the guests.

"But now tell me about the children, Stella?" The young mother looks lovingly at her baby. "I'm sorry, again I can't help you. Right now she really wants to drink. "

"Do n't worry about that . But this is not really a job, it's fun to pamper your guests a little . I'm just a little worried that your husband might want to take you to Dresden with him tonight. Did he mention anything during the short call? "

"No, he hasn't said anything about that yet. He estimates he's with us around 5:00 p.m. I don't even know whether he's coming in a camper or by car. It's hard to believe that we've only talked briefly on the phone twice since she is born. The boss seems to have to put him on the curb , so much overtime! And to the many photos of Katharina, which I sent him on his cell phone, he didn't react as I expected. Any normal father would be delighted with such a cute daughter. "

"Yes, one would have to assume that. But I really believe that it's just the stress that has kept him from telling you what he is really feeling so far. This afternoon, when he takes you in his arms and sees his sweet daughter, you will surely notice how much he loves you both. "

Melanie takes the baby from her breast. "She wasn't thirsty. Now she fell asleep. Maybe she just wanted to suckle a little . Everyone else is totally in love with Katrinchen. Even Benno is completely blown away by her, and I'm curious what Mario will say about his little niece. I'm a little disappointed with Gregor's reaction. Can you understand this?"

"Of course I can understand that. But I am trying to find an explanation for his behavior. First he had this long journey in the motorhome, then he had to work right back into the night, for a few days, and today, on Sunday, he left early to come to you. It's all a bit stressful. And of course the whole thing is very new to him. He probably didn't really follow the pregnancy because he had to work so much. And now he's suddenly a father, which may not be so easy for some men. "

Melanie puts the baby back in the basket. "So now I can still help you a little, luckily. But the more I think about it, I really wonder if Gregor was really looking forward to the baby. Yes, maybe he's just not the person who can express his feelings so directly. After all, his hard work shows that he wants to look after us very well, for me and the baby. "

Stella folds small water lilies out of the napkins. "We'll wait for everything first. Surely he'll come up here this time. Then I can at least take a closer look at it. But now we are completely off the topic. You asked me how it was at the children's service. And I have to tell you, I'm totally excited. It has given me so much happiness , to tell the four girls and two boys of how much joy it can do if it is compatible after an argument again, when you shake hands and says to each other: Everything is fine again, we want to forget everything that was between us. The little ones understood that really well and they even found their own examples. They had a lot of fun with the pictures, too, and I had the feeling that they like to be told nice stories, even if they have a special meaning. I felt that it was a good job to be done with the children on Sunday mornings. "

" So you've now decided to do it every Sunday?"

A smile crosses Stella's face. "Yes I will. On Wednesdays it's I have then to prepare and on Sundays go to church. In addition , I have already received a new offer for a leisure activity. A customer approached me yesterday morning. "

"What is it then? Does it have something to do with the hats you make. "

"No not at all. It is a small private theater company, men and women who dance a type of ballet to classical music. The initiator is a pianist who also wrote the entire choreography. Everyone has to sew their own costumes and the first appearance is planned for autumn. Until then, rehearsals will always take place on Thursday evenings. In the cellar of this woman from Hüttendorf. She is a widow, and because she has always been alone a lot since then, she started many groups. A group that plays pantomimes, some small music groups with different instruments, a folk dance group and this group for expressive dances, as they call them. "

"And why did you choose this ballet group and nothing from the other offers?"

"Unfortunately I don't play an instrument and the pantomime group isn't looking for anyone at the moment. This expression is currently not in great demand, not in the way that Frau von Hüttendorf offers it. So I thought I just want to try it out. "

"That sounds good, if I weren't so tired from the disturbed nights, I would have a good desire to participate. Well, I notice that I'm much too tired to go to Dresden with Gregor tonight. I hope he's taken time off so he can stay here one night. Tomorrow everything may be better. But I'd like to stay here a few more days. "

" Stay as long as you want! I think Gregor has just as little time for you in Dresden as he used to. Then you just feel alone. And now for the first time we can certainly still help you, Mario, Benno and me. At least wait until you've gotten back on your feet a bit! "

"Thanks to you I already am , Stella. When I sit here on your balcony and look at your little paradise, I can relax wonderfully. But the walks with you here in the nearby forest also make me particularly happy . It was always only a few steps, but I liked the spring flowers that grow wild in the forest , everything you showed me out there among the ferns and mosses. I have never looked at any herb that closely before. And what you know about it, all of your explanations about bionics, that really fascinated me. "

The bell in the hall is noticeable.

A little later Benno appears at the door, packed with a few different packages and a bouquet of flowers. He has brought a large, colorful spring bouquet for Stella and Melanie, a cake platter full of pieces of cake and a few small parcels which he gives to the young mother.

Melanie packs tiny baby shoes out of the wrapping paper and a little cuddly bear.

"You absolutely have to become a godfather," suggests the young woman. "And not just because of the gifts, but because you think so lovingly about the little one. I thank you for that, you picked out really cute things. Katharina will definitely love the bear very much when she is a little bigger. "

"Not worth mentioning," says Benno. "Can I maybe help you a little?"

Stella puts the flowers in a large vase. "If you like , you can put the cake pieces on the coffee table. I just put the coffee in the large thermos bottle so that we can chat comfortably and undisturbed . "

Benno looks at the baby in love. "She's getting prettier every day. If you really want me to be your godfather, I would be proud. Your husband is coming this afternoon, then we can finally get to know each other. "

He watches attentively as Melanie changes the baby. "It's not that difficult," he notes. " Perhaps you will let me do that afterwards . I promise you to be extra careful too. "

Melanie smiles. " I already trust you to be careful. And you are welcome to try it once. At the moment she needs a fresh diaper all the time. "

While the two are busy with Katharina, the doorbell rings again. Stella goes to the door, her heart is beating fast with excitement . She is annoyed about it and takes a deep breath. Just don't be so nervous , it's just Mario. She tries to convince herself that she doesn't feel any excitement and takes several deep breaths before opening the apartment door.

Mario is carrying two bouquets of flowers that almost cover his face. The one with the velvety glut fragrant red roses, he gives Stella.

She looks at him a little embarrassed. "Hello, nice to have you here, have you got over your cold? Your sister and Benno, they're waiting for you too. And of course your little niece Katharina. You will immediately fall in love with her. "

Obviously that was the wrong keyword. "I will definitely find her very cute, Stella. But I am especially in love with you. You will never forget that. And it will always stay that way. "

"Let's not talk about it today, Mario!" She asks him. "You know , that I have my problems with that. But we still want to have a nice afternoon today, we've already prepared everything for it. "

The young man also hands her a large packet of cakes. "I brought lemon rolls especially for you. You really like them. Or has your taste changed? "

She smiles and shakes her head. "No, my taste doesn't change that quickly. But come in, you are expected. And we are all so in love with your niece that you have to get in line to be able to poke her around. "

First he follows her into the kitchen, helps her to garnish the cake on a cake plate and then storms into the living room, where he first greets his sister and then the baby. He rocks his little niece in his arms for a few minutes, his eyes beaming happily.

He politely extends his hand to Benno, watching him carefully from head to toe . The two men look each other in the eye, questioningly and searchingly.

I have to defuse the situation a little, Stella thinks, and interferes. "If you stand there for a longer time , even the coffee in the thermos will get cold," she jokes. "We finally want to celebrate the birth of this sweet little baby and toast with non-alcoholic sparkling wine in honor of the proud, pretty mother." She hands the three guests the sparkling drink in the fine, slim glasses.

"That's a reason to celebrate," says Mario. "After all, I became an uncle of this charming Katharina."

They let the glasses sound tenderly together and wish good health and a happy future for the baby.

After the drink, they gather at the living room table and try the various cakes that are appetizingly tempting.

Katharina sleeps in the little basket that is next to the sofa and doesn't seem to notice anything.

"I didn't think you'd have your child here," says Mario happily. "You couldn't do me a bigger favor at the moment. I couldn't have visited you so quickly in Dresden . I hope , you will stay a little longer here. I'm sure I'll be able to miss Gregor for a few more days. He always has so much work to do anyway. "

"I also hope that I can stay here a little longer," says Melanie. "I am so well looked after by Stella and Benno, also by the nice midwife who comes by here every day, that I have already thought about staying a little longer. And after all, you're around here, too, and now you can visit me more often after having overcome the cold. "

"You can suggest Gregor look for a job here . Why does it have to be Dresden? Good auto mechanics are wanted everywhere. We could then help each other a little, especially now that you would be there alone with the baby, because Gregor doesn't have time "

Melanie sighed. "It's always about the dear money. He's so hardworking. I have to be sensible, because he's only doing everything to look after us well. I really can't complain about that. But the idea is not a bad one. Bonn is also a very nice city. Not as beautiful as Dresden for a long time, but at the moment it's more about practical ideas. "

Mario nods eagerly. "I'll talk to my brother-in-law in a moment and show him the advantages, which would be particularly favorable for both of you here in Bonn. After all, you have no more relatives there, and as far as I know, Gregor has no longer anyone there to make him stay in Dresden. "

Melanie grimaces and looks at her brother with sad eyes. "Dresden is a beautiful city and Gregor was born there. And the longer I think about it, the less I think he wants to move from there. The way I see it, his buddies there are all the ones he works with. But I'll definitely talk to him sometime. Quite apart from that, I hope to see all three of you soon to be baptized in Dresden. There is nothing against registering three godparents for little Katharina. What do you think?"

Mario smiles. "I expected that from you."

Benno looks a little embarrassed at the young mother. "I don't know if I can accept that. After all, I'm not related, and we haven't known each other that long either. Do you really want to place such trust in me? "

Melanie beams at him . "Of course, you and Stella, you were my two greatest helpers before and during the birth. I don't know what else I would have done without you. "

Stella takes the young mother in her arms. "I thank you, dear! I am really proud to be a godmother. Of course, I do not want you to influence, but certainly we could help you with Katharina much better if you are here. But of course that is your own decision, and if you stay in Dresden, then we will arrange it certainly as good as possible for us to visit you , as often as we can, and be there for you in all ways. "

Benno takes his glass. "We want to toast one more time. No matter how you decide and where you live: To the sponsorship! "

When the glasses clink gently together, Katharina stirs in her basket and begins to cry softly. Melanie jumps up, picks up the little girl and rocks her back and forth. "Please excuse me for a moment , she's hungry."

Just as she closes the bedroom door behind her, the doorbell rings on the apartment door. Stella opens the door and looks at two policemen who are looking at her questioningly. They both hold out a hand to her with an ID card.

"We received the message that a Melanie Globisch is visiting you. Can we speak to you once, please? "

Stella is startled. "The jewel theft!" Shoots the young woman in the head. " Something must have come out about the company by now. Perhaps now all employees will be interrogated? Did you even arrest someone? Poor Melanie! Hopefully she isn't too upset now. "

She says: "Yes, please come in with me! Take a seat in the living room! I'll get my friend right away, she's just breastfeeding her baby. It was only born a few days ago. "

One of the two policemen gave a startled cry. "Oh, I'm sorry! And now we have to come here with news like this. "The two men follow Stella into the living room, where Benno offers them coffee.

The officers refuse and stop in front of the living room table. The hostess hurries into the next room to the young mother .

When Stella returns with Melanie, the two women expect to find out more about the theft, the company and the employees there. The young mother expects the worst. Was Gregor even falsely arrested?

After a short greeting, Melanie looks at the police officers questioningly: " Has something happened?

The whole thing is definitely just a mistake. I guess that there is something incorrect."

The tall officer looks down. "I'm sorry, Ms. Globisch! Unfortunately there is no mistake. Her husband had a car accident a few hours ago. And although the rescue workers were on the spot very quickly, he could no longer be rescued. It is impossible to mix them up, we found his identity card, and he has also been identified by a colleague at work. "

Melanie stares at the officer with wide eyes. "What are you telling me now ?! That cant be true. He comes with the motorhome, so he always drives it very carefully. And you can't go that fast with it. No, that must be a mistake, Gregor is alive. "

The policeman rocks his head slightly and says with a regretful look: "We are really sorry not to be able to bring you better news. Her husband , Gregor Globisch, did not drive the mobile home , because his own car was not intact, he drove with a colleague's sports car, Mr. Anton Ziegler. He had kindly lent him the car so that he could come to you as soon as possible. Unfortunately, an error is really impossible. "

Melanie still looks at him blankly. "I just can't believe that. That can't be true. "She looks around, looks at us individually. "What do you think about that, that's not possible. Do you think so? Maybe these are fake policemen and they just want to scare me . "

One of the officers shows her the ID card. "You are welcome to call the police or come to the nearest service center with your friends . They will unfortunately confirm this terrible accident . Please believe us, we are very, very sorry to bring you these news. Your friend told us that you recently had a baby. It is very terrible for you to find out now that your husband has passed away. "

Melanie opens her eyes. "Gregor is supposed to be dead? He has not yet seen his daughter. No, that is definitely not true. He has to see his child , he wanted to be here around 5:00 p.m. and is looking forward to his baby. This is definitely a mix-up. "

"Do you dare to look at a photo of the accident on which you can recognize your husband? I have a photo here on my phone. May be you want or you also prefer to wait until you have fully understood those terrible thoughts. "

"I want to see the photo," she says. "It can't be Gregor at all. He'll ring the doorbell right here. "She snatches the cell phone out of the officer's hand and looks at the photo, which shows an injured man.

Only a fraction of a second passes, the young woman sinks silently into Mario's arms and loses consciousness.

***

12th chapter

Stella and Mario drag the suitcases to the apartment in the apartment building on Kiefernweg , where the young hatter lives. Melanie carries the baby up the numerous steps and holds it close to her . Moni hops happily behind.

"It's good to be back here in your apartment," notes the young mother and looks at Stella gratefully . "Those were exhausting and very sad days in Dresden. And worst of all, the funeral that I feared so much is now over. But I still can't understand it. I feel like I'm in a bad dream, a nightmare that I want to wake up from soon. And again and again I wish Gregor had set off with the mobile home. But now nothing can be changed, even if I keep telling myself that I shouldn't have gone to Bonn. "

"You are not to blame!" Says Mario firmly. "You couldn't have stayed in Dresden, you were there all alone, and maybe then who knows what would have happened to you. It was right that he drove you to Bonn, you were safe here and the birth could go well in the clinic. This is the only way to have a healthy daughter now. Unfortunately, there is evidence that your husband drove way too fast, and there was also a lot of residual alcohol in his blood. That was more than reckless. In that state he shouldn't have been driving a car. So you don't to blame yourself at all. He was a grown man, he shouldn't have acted so negligently . And think about it, luckily no other people were drawn into the accident. Imagine if there had been more deaths due to his irresponsible actions! "

A tear runs down Melanie's cheek. "I do not understand any of this. I haven't understood anything since the day it all happened. Why did he drink so much before ? Why did he take the car? There are so many questions that no one can answer for me. And everything is now locked for the police. Alcohol and a high speed. And no tampering with the car . They say that's enough for them. But I just don't believe it. Something is wrong, don't you think that too, Stella? "

"Do you think it could have something to do with the jewel heist? I can't find any connection there. The police have ruled out third-party negligence. "

Melanie caresses the baby's tender cheeks. It looks , as if she's smiling. "If I didn't have Katharina now, I don't know what I would do . And I don't know what I'd do alone in Dresden either . I am so grateful that I can stay here for the time being, I can't tell you that. Still, I can't shake my suspicion that it might have something to do with the theft. "

"If you care so much about doing more research, then I will definitely help you, dear Melanie. Then

I'll just go to Dresden and spy around a bit. But at the moment I definitely can't leave you here alone. "

"It's way too dangerous for you," says Melanie. "I would never allow you to rummage around there alone in the criminal milieu. No, if something happened to you then I would give myself even more thought and even more reproaches. "

Mario interferes. "I wouldn't allow you to go after the jewel robbers there alone, Stella . If Melanie is better, the three of us can always go back to Dresden and take a look around there. And we have to plan that very well beforehand, because even a tiny mistake could be very dangerous if there really is something to your guess. "

Melanie sighs. "Yes, just think about it . It's all weird. Of course, outwardly, the case is clear. Gregor drove too fast and Gregor had residual alcohol in his blood. But why didn't he drive the camper the way he wanted to? And why was his own car broken down? I didn't know anything about that either. Of course, he never told me everything. But the funny thing is that he has a suspicion and talks about colleagues in the workshop who may have been involved in the robbery. And a few days later he dies in an accident that is still strange to me. Doesn't that seem strange to you? "

"It can also be a coincidence," says Mario, pouring water into three glasses. "Sometimes there are very strange coincidences in life. Anyway, I still have a lot of vacation left. I could spend a few days in Dresden if you have more peace afterwards, little sister. "

"I still have enough vacation", Stella tells them. "I had such thoughts some time ago. I wanted to sneak into the company as a cleaning lady. But maybe that's too noticeable, and in my presence they might all be mute. "

Melanie hugs Katharina tightly and kisses her tenderly. "But I have a better idea. So far the funeral has only taken place in silence, in a very small group. I could write an invitation for a private memorial service for his work colleagues, for everyone in the company. All three of us then take a good look at this appointment . "

Mario empties the water glass "Do you think they're all coming? I think many people will shirk it. Such celebrations are not exactly popular. "

Stella smiles. "Maybe we'll move the celebration to the company. A ceremony right after work and the three of us bring a buffet and a lot of alcohol like catering. They will not be able to resist this offer so easily. We could even take a close look at the boss. "

The other two nod in agreement.

"In any case, we can think about it and plan a little," says Melanie.

The doorbell on the front door answers. The young mother is startled. "Whenever the doorbell rings, I now fear bad news. I got very scared, please excuse me! "

"We can all understand that," says Stella and lets the guest in. It is Benno who is holding some boxes of pizza in his hand. "I once thought that when you come home from the long journey , you are bound to be hungry."

"You guessed it well," Mario praised him. "How have you been in the meantime?"

"I've worked a lot now , as you can probably guess. After I let the work drag a bit through the circumstances, I still had a lot to catch up on. I now have a time for that again and can help you when you need it. Stella has taught me always good to happiness, so I was informed of your very sad activities. "He distributes the pizza boxes, Stella puts napkins and cutlery on the table and asks the others to the table.

"Come on guys! We want to strengthen ourselves first when Benno spoils us here. I am really hungry after the long drive. I hope the rest of you too. "

During the meal, Antonio and Melanie report on the endless conversations with the police and the silent funeral.

"I do not even know , if it was right, if it has been in Gregor's sense. But I just didn't want anyone with me . In any case, no foreigners. And that's why there were only four of us, the pastor, my brother, Stella and I, "she concludes her report.

"If it was all right with you, then Gregor will certainly be happy too," says Benno. It's good that you can relax here for now. And if I were you, I wouldn't worry about the future at the moment. "

"I've already thought about it, Benno. I've already given notice of my apartment there, but I still have to comply with the notice period. I'm going to move here next to my brother. And you are here, my friends, so I think I can get through the next time well. "

" Really good idea," he agrees . " If you want to bring your things here , we can help you move."

"I'll leave most of it there so I don't have to remember everything. I've already spoken to someone who wants to liquidate the apartment for me. I only want a few very private things in my new life here in Bonn. "

"But we can help you with that," he promises.

Melanie looks around. "You are really good friends! My brother included, of course. "

Katharina answers with a quiet cry. "I have to leave you alone now," explains the young mother. "She's definitely hungry. You might think now that I'll jump way too fast if the little one just lets out a peck, but you have to understand me, she's all I have now. I can't help it, I have to pamper her. "

"Nobody blames her," replies Benno. "We all love to pamper your daughter, and everyone understands that you need her very much now, too . But don't worry, she needs you a lot now. You are everything for her now. "

"And of course she also has you , after all, you will be her godparents. But with the baptism, I have to take my time now. I can't do that at the moment. It's just too emotional a celebration. Can you understand that? "

Benno nods. "It was all too much for you now anyway. It is good that you are here with Stella now. First you can calm down and cope with everything a bit. It is the best to always listen to your gut instinct in the future. Only do what is good for you. "

"I'll make sure of that," promises Stella. "And now go , and don't worry too much about anything, and certainly not about us. Katharina already has a name, and God loves her so much, even if she has not yet been baptized in church. "

"That's true," adds Mario. "God also loves unbaptized children, children of all religions and also those of the Gentiles. When you are ready one day, Katrinchen will be carried to church. But it doesn't matter if she walks to her baptism on her own two feet. "

***

13th chapter

The mild evening sun shines through the colored curtain and the window and bathes the room in a pastel-colored, colorful light. Mario sets up the new cot for Katharina in Stella's guest room.

Stella helps him and hands him the screws and tools.

"We are a good team," says Mario, beaming at the young woman.

"W e are a great team," agrees Stellas. "Your sister keeps telling me how glad she is that we are all helping. But she bears everything so bravely. Unfortunately, her little daughter keeps her busy around the clock. "

"Yeah, she doesn't have much to think about. Perhaps she is pushing out a lot now when she is busy. But what do you think of us now? We found a new way to each other again in these terrible hours. Or how do you see that?"

"Melanie needs both of us, and I also believe that we will be great to help her in this way. But that doesn't mean that we're both automatically a couple again, even if we spend a lot of time together now. "

He looks at her pleadingly "But what do your feelings say?"

" Please don't ask me about it now. Right now, it's really my job to comfort your sister. She alone matters now with her great grief. Such a young couple, yes, a young family , is torn apart so suddenly , so cruelly, that I now put my own problems and feelings very far behind. The two of us, you and me, just don't matter that much now . Can you understand this?"

"Yes, of course I can understand that. I'm also hurt when I see , how Melanie suffers. But I just thought, I can see that Benno also feels something for you. I'm just afraid of losing you completely. "

Stella sighs. "Oh, Mario! I beg you! You can only lose something that you own. We don't have a relationship, you know that. But I know, of course , what you mean. You are afraid that I will fall in love with Benno, or maybe you want to know now whether I am in love with him or not? "

He looks at her tenderly. "Yes, maybe this is not the right moment because we both want to be there for Melanie. But of course I'm afraid that you will fall in love with Benno. Do you feel nothing for me anymore? "

"Believe me, right now I'm not even thinking about love. And I don't inquire into my feelings either. Of course I have felt something for you until now, after all, you were my great love. Otherwise it wouldn't have hurt so much. And because it hasn't hurt that much lately, I assumed that love isn't that great either. "

"I think one has nothing to do with the other, Stella. I 'm still so sorry for everything I've done to you in the past . And I would like to undo it. But unfortunately that is not possible. I would also like to prove to you that I am convinced that this will never happen again, and I hope that we can now build a good trust in one another. I'm so grateful for your help, for all that you do for my sister. But maybe you can still tell me if I can have a little bit of hope. "

Stella looks at the finished cot. "That looks pretty nice. It is a pleasure to do something with you. And now I enjoy being with you again. But at the moment I am afraid to continue researching my feelings . If it calms me down, I haven't had any feelings of love for Benno either. At the moment I only feel friendship for him, maybe you should know that. "

Mario breathes again. "Oh, thank you, that takes away my fear for the moment. I feel every day that I love you so much. And I also know that this condition will always last. Do you feel like doing something with me? Maybe you would like to go dancing with me one day? "

"Really not at the moment, Mario. The shock is still somehow in my limbs. First this beautiful event with the birth, then the shock with Gregor's death, and now this not entirely unfounded suspicion about the accident, which perhaps wasn't an accident after all. Melanie already made me think when she said it was strange that Gregor's death came so soon after the jewel was robbed . That is circling around in my mind the whole time , and I can't really distract myself. "

"Maybe it's good if you distract yourself from time to time. You used to love to dance so much. And what happened to your wishes with the ballet? You even stopped the thing with the children's church service for now. You are about to set up your whole life just on my sister. Not that I don't allow my sister to do this! I wish her the best too. But I am worried about you because you are so self-sacrificing. "

"Maybe you're right, maybe it's really some kind of escape for me. Or maybe it's just a way of coming to terms with all of these terrible events. Everything is much worse for Melanie than it is for me. And everything is still so fresh and so new. Just let some time pass, please! "

He looks at her with wide eyes. "Of course! If you want that, I'll try to understand that too. And tell me if I get on your nerves. Because I definitely don't want that, that I 'm around too much and that I disturb you. "

"You definitely don't bother. No, I feel really good with you, and I think that time will bring everything, Mario. "

"Do we want to take Moni for a walk in the woods tonight?" He suggests.

"No, and please understand! I have an appointment with Benno. He looks forward to walking the dog every evening. I also enjoy this evening walk into nature, it builds me up after the stress of everyday life, this view of the green and the chirping of birds. And I don't want to refuse Benno, because he has done so much for all of us and helps us , wherever he can. He even helped your sister . "

Mario nods. "I know that, and I'm very grateful to him for that. He is also a wonderful godfather to Katharina. I am always amazed at how skillfully he handles the leash, even though it is so tiny. He really does it as well as a father. There have been moments when I wished that he would fall in love with Melanie and she would fall in love with her . The two would be a good couple and a real family. "

Stella grimaces. "But with your wishes you are way ahead of your time. I can't imagine your sister overcoming her grief so quickly and falling in love so fast. That wouldn't be normal. I think at the moment she is still in the phase where she cannot even grasp the death of her husband. I think it's good that we're planning to investigate all of these suspicions in Dresden. She then has the opportunity to gradually understand, grasp and maybe even process everything. "

Melanie enters the room. "Oh, you two have been busy. I could never have done it alone. May I invite you to dinner now? Kathi is sleeping now and the lasagne has just finished. I've cheated a little, it's not entirely homemade. I bought the pastry sheets ready-made and I also used a ready-made sauce for the filling. I only seasoned and steamed meat and vegetables myself. The bechamel sauce, on the other hand, is out of the bag. I hope you still like it. "

"I'm really hungry," announces Mario. "And like everything , that you cooked in recent times, has great taste. Only your initial skills a few years ago, there wasn't that good you could have build a house with these. "

Melanie gives him a light pat. "I was still half a child then and really had no idea. But at least I've tried and I've been improving ever since. And now come quickly, because the little one is still sleeping. We can eat there without me having to stop to breastfeed. "

Stella and the two siblings go to the dining area of the living room, where the young mother has set the table. The steaming lasagne is in a bowl in the middle of the table. Another guest arrives, it's Benno, who brings some baby things and offers to help. Melanie invites him to have a bite to eat, too , and he happily and gratefully agrees. The four of them take a seat in the dining area, and Melanie says grace .

When she is done, she looks at Mario. "I thought about introducing this ritual again. After all, I now have a responsibility to my young daughter and I want to show her the right way through life. This also means that I make her the offer to turn to God at any time. I said a prayer of thanks when Katrinchen was born and also a prayer when the pediatrician told me that she was a very healthy child. And now I want to try to talk to God so that he explains to me why Gregor had to go. I cannot understand that in the normal way. "

"What a nice idea," says Stella. "A person will not be able to answer any of your questions. One of them will say you can be lucky or unlucky in life. The good one likes to take, but with all the terrible fates that befall one, you always wonder , why. There are people who perceive a difficult fate as a punishment or at least as something that tries to annoy them or make them unhappy. And it is also a fact that unhappiness and sadness can neither be avoided nor suppressed. Somehow you have to go through it, and I've always had the experience that the best way to do this is to ask God. Sometimes he would give me a very clear answer through someone, or I would find something in the Bible or in some other document. "

"I also think your idea is very good, Melanie," agrees Benno. "Unfortunately we live in a completely different world that is not as good as we would like it to be. And if we really want to find out whether there is more to the accident, then we need a whole lot: a lot of good common sense and caution. But also all sorts of bad thoughts so that we can put ourselves in the shoes of the perpetrators. And then of course a whole host of Guardian Angels. Unfortunately, I can't help you that much because I hardly have any vacation days and that's why I suggest that I take care of Moni while you are in Dresden, so that you can work there undisturbed. A dog could seriously disturb you in secret investigations. "

Stella looks at him happily "If that isn't get too much for you, Benno, then I'll accept your offer. As much as I would like to have him with me, my dog, it will be difficult in our research to always keep him quiet somewhere. If you take care of him here in the meantime, then I am reassured because I know that Moni feels at home with you and that she likes it. "

As if she had understood, the dog runs to Benno and licks the back of his hand briefly.

Mario looks at Benno. "You don't want to come along?" His voice sounds somewhat relieved.

" Unfortunately I ca n't. Otherwise I would love to help you. But I don't know if I would be a good detective either. And I don't consider myself very diplomatic either. What are you going to do now? "

"We drive to Dresden on the first day when Mario is on vacation. I will organize a kind of farewell party for Gregor at the company. I've already discussed everything with the boss. Stella, Mario and I are preparing a buffet that we will bring with us this afternoon. And I've ordered a lot of beer and other drinks from a beverage company. We will take a close look at Gregor's colleagues and, speak and mingle a little with the people. Maybe there is some indication of something inconsistent. "

"Even if it was really an accident, at least you tried everything. Then at least you are safe and one can slowly process this terrible event. Can't you get a detective to help you there can you? "

"If we don't get anywhere on our own, we will definitely seek professional help," promises Mario. "Above all, I don't want the two women to be in danger here. As soon as there is anything suspicious during the celebration, I will send them both home and do further research or call the police. "

Benno breathes a sigh of relief. "That's good, Mario, I was a bit worried. If it wasn't an accident, then you might be among criminals. And if an employee is really to blame for this, then you are in great danger. If this guy didn't have any qualms about killing Gregor, then he won't have any qualms about you either. So really just take a look at these people and stay away from them if something is wrong. "

"And how do you like the lasagna now?" Asks Melanie. " You eat like sparrows."

"Oh, I'm sorry," Benno regrets. "It tastes fantastic, but we got pretty angry about these serious and important issues. You're right , we should n't have such serious conversations while eating . I was just worried about you. "

"That's nice of you," says Stella and passes the large bowl around again. "And while we're gone, please tell Moni about me so that she doesn't miss me too much. But I know she is in good hands with you . "

"And if she gets homesick for you, I'll take special vacation and visit you in the beautiful ELBFLORENZ."

***

14th chapter

Hugo, the boss of the company "Autoworks", has distributed several bouquets with white flowers for decoration in the workshop. On the small side table there is a photo of Gregor with a black mourning stripe. While Mario deposits the drinks on a large table, Stella and Melanie decorate the buffet on two other large side tables .

Stella watches the boss out of the corner of her eye . His eyes are narrowing, his mouth is pulled down slightly, a little mockingly. His gait is creeping, reminding the young woman of the striving forward of old cats. She checks her feelings and realizes that something indefinable from her stomach reports that she does not like him.

"Did Gregor tell you something about this Hugo?" She turns to Melanie. "Did he get on well with him?"

"He hardly said anything, but when he did, it wasn't that good. Gregor was always the boss' bogeyman. And whenever something went wrong, he had to play the scapegoat. But if he does not really have anything to do with the jewel robbery, then I can not think as yet no reason one why he the death of should have been to blame my husband. Unless Gregor knew anything about Hugo's criminal machinations. I also have a lot of confidence in him. In any case, I will keep an eye on him to see whether he will cry crocodile tears after the speech, or whether he is genuinely moved. Have you already looked at the others? "

Stella nods. "Yes, especially this Anton, whom your husband must have known a little better. I find him somehow indefinable. And what is your impression of him? "

"I didn't like him back then when he was talking to my husband about the two colleagues. And now I keep thinking about who these two colleagues can be. There are only three left here. There is this Freddy, then Henk and Wolfgang. There isn't anyone else at the moment. So we should find the ones that we can rule out. Who is the least suspicious of them? "

"It's hard to say, Melanie. We have barely exchanged a word with them , except when they were greeted. We just have to watch them as carefully as possible. And Mario will help us with that. "

The young mother nods and looks at the basket in which little Katharina is sleeping.

Wolfgang steps up and looks at the baby. "You have a lovely daughter! I don't even know who she looks more like now, Gregor or you? "

"It always changes from time to time," Melanie knows. "Right now I have the impression that she looks like my mother in her baby photos. Sometimes these similarities come out from the grandparents in between. Of course, I also wish that she inherited something from Gregor, so that later I will have the feeling that something of him lives on in her. But right now these thoughts hurt too much. Surely he was a good colleague, wasn't Gregor? "

"He was a good boy and a good buddy," that's how Wolfgang defines him. "But you know best what kind of person he was. What should I tell you ?! None of us would have thought that our life would end in such a tragic way. We all have a little surprise for you afterwards . But of course none of this can comfort you, I know that very well. Losing a partner so young is a tragic misfortune! My sincere condolences!"

Tears collect in the corner of her eye. She'll have to pull herself together if she doesn't want to use the tissue all the time. So she decides to quickly change the subject. "Thank you, yes! I have to cope with that somehow. At some point I will probably make it. But how are you doing here now? I'm sure you miss my husband very much too. He was a talented specialist, otherwise he wouldn't have been employed so many hours a day here, would he? "

"Of course your husband is irreplaceable", Wolfgang hurries to say. "We were forced to hire Henk here in a hurry so that we could get along with the work. Anton and I, we couldn't have made it any further here on our own. And then I have another request for you! "

"Just say it! Maybe I have the opportunity , to help you with that. Is it maybe a souvenir of my husband? "

" No, it is not. It's a very delicate matter , it's about Anton. Was it he who lent your husband the sports car so quickly so that he could drive to you on Sunday. And then Gregor had an accident with this car. That's why Anton is of course very reproaching himself, and he's really depressed about it. In the beginning I even believed that he would harm himself. Even when the investigation revealed that there was nothing wrong with the car, he continued to reproach himself. So please do not be surprised if he is very embarrassed now and possibly even avoids contact with you a little. He still has a guilty conscience and is afraid to face you. "

"Oh, don't worry, Wolfgang! You always blame yourself. I blame myself and tell myself that the whole thing would not have happened if I hadn't even gone to Bonn. I said again and again, what would have been , though. But Anton only meant well when he lent my husband the car. He's not to blame at all, I'll make that clear to him. It was just a tragic accident and the police found out that he was driving way too fast. Absolutely too fast , and then he panned the steering wheel . Maybe there was some animal on the road or some other obstacle that he had to avoid. But that will remain unexplained forever, because nothing and nobody has been found. And even if there was a deer or something, on this route, in this dangerous stretch, it should never have driven so fast. As sorry as I am, it looks like he was responsible for the accident through his own recklessness. "

"I'm reassured when you see it that way, dear Melanie. We all feared a bit that you might make him partly responsible. Another woman would certainly have done that and would not be as understanding as you! "

"No no! It's OK. I appreciate all of the way you conduct yourself here. It is for this reason that I have decided to hold this celebration here. I've always had the impression that my husband has good colleagues. But now, please excuse me! I have a few little things to finish here. We will certainly talk to each other later and have the opportunity for a few private words. "

"That would be very nice, Melanie. See you later! "He walks away , the young mother hurriedly takes the baby out of the basket, presses it against her and gently rocks it back and forth.

"My poor darling," she whispers in the child's ear. "If I only knew what I am doing here and who I should believe?" She turns to Stella and sighs. "Were you able to look a little at Wolfgang now? What is your impression of him? "

"Unfortunately none yet. But I couldn't understand what he was saying to you either. In between he tripped from one foot to the other a bit nervously and rubbed his fingers so strangely while talking. But in the end he also seems a bit inscrutable to me like everyone here . We just have to keep watching him. "

Melanie tells her friend what concerns Wolfgang has about Anton.

"That sounds interesting," says Stella. "According to the police report, there was really nothing on the car. Or do you think that the appraiser has made common cause with these men? "

"No, I think that's impossible. They were experts from the police, from the Kripo. They are incorruptible and definitely do not work with such a workshop. But then we can definitely rule out this Henk now, because he is new to the team and can actually have nothing to do with the accident. "

"Yes, Melanie. I keep asking myself why we have such strange feelings. They are neither logical nor justified. The police have established perfectly that no third-party fault can be possible. They also found no traces of anyone else in the car, except Anton himself, and he had a waterproof alibi at the time. "

"It's funny with feelings like that, probably an old instinct from the time when people still lived in the great outdoors and had to anticipate dangers. We probably just don't like the men here because they are not on the same wavelength as us. You don't have to be criminals, Stella. "

"Right, they are just normal auto mechanics, skilled people who are trained to find and eliminate errors. Are you ready now? "

"Yes, I've now finished everything, we can start."

As if called, the company's employees gather in the large room with Hugo, the boss, and join Stella,

Melanie and Mario, who set up the drinks buffet in the meantime.

First the boss gives a little speech. He greets those present and expresses his thanks, especially that this memorial service can take place in his rooms. This is followed by a speech in which he praises Gregor's services and presents the audience with a brief life story of the deceased.

The two women wipe the tears from the corners of their eyes, and the faces of the others who are present also look affected and touched.

A decent applause shows that all the words of thanks and praise are recognized and confirmed.

Melanie also gives a short speech and thanks the company boss and his employees for the sympathy and the opportunity of this memorial hour.

She concludes with the words. "I am quite sure that Gregor is now watching us from heaven, and I now cordially invite you to serve you food and drinks at the buffet."

Mario hands everyone a champagne glass, raises his and says solemnly: "To Gregor, my brother-in-law, my sister's husband and your colleagues and employees!"

Everyone raises their glass. "To Gregor!" It sounds from all sides.

While Stella is talking to the boss to get to know him a little better, Melanie turns to Anton. "I'm very sorry about this. So, I mean you kindly lent my husband your car to help him out. And then this terrible accident! I can imagine that you are not very happy about it. "

Anton nods vigorously. "You hit the nail on the head. I've been blaming myself every day since it happened. I wouldn't have lent him the car if I hadn't known that he used to drive car races. So I assumed that he could handle my sports car well.

He was also the one in the workshop who always repaired this type of car and then also tested it. But I didn't consider that he was in such a hurry to go to Bonn. I'm really so sorry. "

Melanie looks at him with big eyes. "I like to believe you. But you really don't have to blame yourself, it was his decision to go that fast. I knew that he was repairing racing cars and tested them. But not that he also raced himself . He never told me about that either. "

"Well, it was more of a private race. But once or twice he was also on a real racetrack, more for fun. He liked it a lot back then, it was quite a while ago. He was a good driver, I would never have believed him to steer the car into the abyss at this point. Have you already seen this place? "

"No. The police only showed me one photo. To go there, I haven't been able to do that until now. I didn't have the strength to do that, and it would hurt too much. But at some point later I will erect a memorial cross there. I've already made up my mind. "

"You don't have to do that. We all got together and put up a small cross there and put flowers and candles. Finally we are all still very shocked, it came so suddenly. I congratulated him on the baby and wished him a good trip. And when I saw the heap of scrap that was lying at the bottom of the slope, I couldn't understand it at all. "

" And what about the car now, Anton?"

"It's really just a pile of tin. This was fully insured, because it was still new . And the appraisers examined it again and again, but found no defect. The pace was too fast for this corner and nobody knows why he panned the steering wheel. Maybe he wanted to light a cigarette. But none was found. Maybe he was so overtired that he fell asleep. Or an animal just ran across the street and overreacted.

No one saw something of human souls far and wide. "

"Who knew everything that he would drive this route?" Asks Melanie.

" Everyone in the company knew that he wanted to be there on Sunday . So the boss and his daughter and we colleagues. But nobody except me knew that he would be driving the sports car. I only offered him that an hour before departure. Why is this important to you? "

"I would like to reconstruct the last day before his death. I would like to know why he was so overtired. "

"I think he was very sleepy. He hadn't slept much all the nights before. He worked way too long every night. But don't think that the boss asked him to do that. He was a real workhorse and he couldn't stop once it was his turn. He always wanted to satisfy the customers who all wanted their car back quickly. You probably know that too, most people bring their car and then want it back the next day if possible. He was just too good for the world, your husband. "

Melanie is startled. "If you say that! I probably didn't know him very well because we rarely saw each other. In fact, we've only known each other three years, during which he worked most of the time. That was certainly not enough. But you were with him for many hours a day. You must have known him much better. "

Anton looks at the photo with the black ribbon. "He was okay, Gregor. You could steal horses with him. We will all keep him in good memory. Wait a minute! Now we have to pause briefly. I just see the boss who is there with the surprise for you. I hope that you will be happy! "

Hugo asks those present to hear, he holds a thick envelope and asks Melanie to come over. He solemnly pushes the envelope into her hand. "This is a small donation from all of us together. We collected because we are so sorry for the whole story. Of course this is only a drop in the ocean and it certainly cannot comfort you in your grief, but maybe it will be a little help in difficult times and you can use it to fulfill small wishes for yourself and your daughter. It's not a secret here either , so I can tell you what amount you will find in it. It's exactly 10,000 euros. "

Melanie is startled. "For heaven's sake! So much money! But that's not possible, I can't accept that. "

Hugo takes her hand. " Of course you can accept that. We have collected that together and really like to give it away. We all benefited greatly from Gregor. He was a good employee, a good colleague, he really helped everyone, and we are still grateful to him for everything he has done. Take it and make good use of it! You can accept it with a clear conscience. We will not be poor because of it. "

Melanie is still trying to find the right words. "I really didn't expect that now. I am so touched and of course so grateful. In fact, as a young widow I certainly can't make big steps now. Fortunately, besides my brother Mario, I also have very dear friends in Bonn, here my friend Stella, who is also such a great help to me, every day. She reshaped her whole life to help me. All this , she has rebuilt just in her life, she neglected, so I feel good and Katharina. I don't even know what to say now. And now you are all so nice to me! "She wipes the tears that run down her cheeks with the tissue and looks at him gratefully .

The emotion overwhelmed her , she thanks the boss and the employees again and then sinks down on a chair, exhausted. Mario joins her and provides her with drinks and food.

Meanwhile, Stella turns to Freddy. "You also knew the deceased well?"

The addressee shook his head. "Unfortunately not that good . I worked in the goods department , but not very long. We also sell spare parts here, and that works quite well because many people repair the cars themselves or have friends help them. There is a lot to do every day in the spare parts store, and we are connected to an assembly line, the workshop and my work area. So if something is needed there, the mechanic calls me and orders his goods, which I send him back on the assembly line. We don't have a regular lunch break, we prefer to do it individually so that we don't have to interrupt our work. We , Gregor and I, haven't had a long conversation so far, so I can't say much about him. He was always nice and friendly and we greeted each other politely when we saw each other. Sometimes thrown a few words or a joke while passing each other. In the evenings we stopped working at different times, so we had little opportunity to get to know each other better. "

"It's a shame," thinks the young woman. "I didn't even know him. I'm just his wife's friend and unfortunately I can't share memories with her because I lived so far away. As you can imagine, I always hopes for people who can tell me a little more about the deceased. "

Freddy ponders for a moment. "Lately I've seen Gregor with Anton and Wolfgang a lot. Now and then they were probably in a pub in Dresden Neustadt and had a beer there together. And at the last Christmas party, Nadja, the boss's daughter, talked a little longer with Gregor. I don't know if they know each other a little better. Not , that there is something bad behind but it was suspect! I just wanted to have said that in general. "

"Oh, that's nice. I have a little clue. Melanie will be leaving her apartment here in the future, with our help. Then we might have the opportunity to talk to some of Gregor's friends. Is this Nadja otherwise available here? "

"She often helps out here in business, in the office of course. But she no longer lives with her father, but has her own apartment near the Golden Rider in Dresden Neustadt. All you have to do is walk across the Elbe bridge, straight ahead, and you're there. I was already at the door of her apartment when the boss asked me to bring her some documents. I don't know them well and I can't say anything about them. You have to form your own judgment about them. "

Stella is startled. That does n't sound particularly friendly. He probably doesn't have a good opinion of her if he is so emphatically neutral. It can't hurt to take a closer look at them. "Do you have her address?"

"Of course, and so does her phone number. I'm sure she regrets not being able to be here today. Gregor has been working here for a few years now, so the two must have known each other a little longer. I'll write everything down for you afterwards, "he promises. "And then again thank you very much for the beautiful invitation and the buffet."

After everyone has reached the buffet again , the staff say goodbye and wish Melanie and her friends all the best. Hugo turns to the young mother. "Can I still be any help to you?"

"That's friendly, but the three of us get along really well. We just have to pack up quickly, then we're gone and you can close the workshop. "

While Stella, Melanie and Mario pack up and clean up, Hugo is still busy in the office. In the workshop

, everyone indulges their thoughts and tries to process the impressions . Freddy takes a quick look and hands Stella the promised note with Nadja's address and telephone number .

"And?" Melanie turns to the two fellow travelers a little later. "Are we a little smarter now? Does anybody have an idea?"

The two look at each other a bit perplexed. "I couldn't find anything suspicious," says Mario.

"I still have to think about that," explains Stella. "And I have to sort out my feelings first. But so far we are really not further. "

***

15th chapter

Luise, the innkeeper, puts a large beer on the table for Mario and Stella. "That's on the house", decides Luise. "After all, Gregor, your friend and brother-in-law, was a regular of mine , and I'm always damned sorry for that. I had read about this accident in the newspaper, but his name wasn't there and there wasn't a picture of him, so I didn't know that it was a guest of mine. You can hardly imagine it when such a young person is torn from life. "

"You can always relax very well with a beer after work," claims Stella. "That is a good thing. And sometimes you can talk about your problems from your soul. Surely his work mates were here with him sometimes, or did he have other friends? "

The landlady sits down next to them for a moment. "They all had a good relationship in the past, that was Anton, Wolfgang, Gregor and a few other colleagues from the workshop. But when the others left the company and only Anton and Wolfgang came here with Gregor, the relationship was no longer as close as it was before. "

"No?" Wonders Mario. "What could have been the reason? Did they fight? "

Luise nods. "Yes, Wolfgang and Anton, very shortly before this terrible accident. Gregor was always here alone the last few evenings. On one day Wolfgang came to this directory, and has quite been bleats him the next day of Anton. I did not understand , what they said, but the sound wasn't friendly, and Gregory seemed to be very worried. Maybe it was because of Nadja. "

"Why is it because of Nadja? Was she here too? "Asks Stella, surprised.

"No. But she used to be with Anton , and then she fell in love with Gregor. But he married Melanie afterwards. She didn't like that, but Anton was happy cause Gregor was out of competition. And yet, Nadja didn't come back to him. I can't say for sure, but I got the impression that she is still after Gregor. He sometimes made such hints when he had drunk a lot. "

Mario looks attentively at Luise. "Did you remember what he said?"

"If he drank too much, he said I can no longer see this burdock. Why doesn't she get it that it's all over? And when he was sober, he spoke often of late nothing but starred only in his glass. "

"Did you hear why Anton and Wolfgang were no longer satisfied with his friendship? Or do you have any idea what it might be about? "

Luise shook her head. "No, really not. They were all just threats with empty words, not facts. The other day he was in a good mood , Gregor . He'd had a lot of schnapps by then. Then he said to me: Luise, if I ever win the lottery, then you can choose something wonderful. But maybe I don't even have to win the lottery, maybe I'll soon have a great inheritance "."

"Did he have someone in his family who is very old or sick and has a fortune?"

"No idea! Surely his wife should know that. I never knew anything about loved ones. I always thought he was an orphan and that he had no siblings. But I can also be wrong. Sometimes the drunk don't tell the truth here either. I have stopped doing a long time to believe anything , what I hear. There's a lot of boasting here, a lot of fantasy stories and pipe dreams. But now I have to keep working. I can't tell you more, I don't know any more. "

Stella and Mario thank Luise and leave the small pub .

The young woman looks up at the cloudy sky. "Couldn't Gregor have expected hush money from the gang who stole the jewels? Could it be what he implied with the alleged lottery win or with the inheritance? "

"I think there are a lot of people who dream of winning the lottery or an inheritance. That doesn't have to mean anything. Are we going a little further along the Elbe? "

Stella's eyes light up. "Oh yes, I love the Elbe promenade. You can really relax a bit there. I love to see the old steamers, and the water laps so peacefully here. "

Mario breathes again. "I'm really happy about that. It worried me very much that you had thrown yourself so much into the work for my sister lately, and I made so many reproaches to myself that I even bothered you with it. "

"Oh nonsense! You really are an idiot, but a nice one. It's really no effort, and I really enjoy doing all of this for Melanie. I like her. She became a friend of mine. "

"And for that you now neglect your friend Silvia very much, the poor! In the children's church service, they have probably already written you off because you are always taking care of my sister. You cancelled your ballet company, even your walks in the forest, where you usually get so much strength , even for that you have currently no time. "

Stella smiles. "What is wrong with you?! We are currently taking a walk in the most beautiful city in Germany. What more can I ask for ?! "

Mario threatens her with his finger. "I always thought that you thought Bonn is the most beautiful city in Germany. Are you going to be unfaithful to Beethoven's birthplace? "

Stella shakes her head happily. "Bonn is still not a big city. Bonn is a cozy little place with an interesting history and a magical flair. But you can't compare it with the colossal art treasures of this historic big city. "

"... which now has a few art treasures less," adds Mario.

"Which brings us back to the topic. We absolutely have to find out whether Anton and Wolfgang have anything to do with the art theft. Perhaps they injected the robbers with the getaway car and received hush money for it. "

Mario suddenly stops. "It's strange that the people in the company can raise a donation of 10,000 euros. It's kind of suspicious too. Well, of course you do n't know who donated how much . Maybe the boss bought most of it. And he seems to have money. When I had a quick chat with Freddy, he told me that Hugo owns a large mansion outside of town. I do believe that you can make a lot of money with a car repair shop. "

"Yes, we absolutely have to find out who donated what. On the other hand, don't you think it would have seemed suspicious to Hugo if one of his employees had donated several thousand euros ?! "

"There's something to it, Stella. Somehow we get stuck. But what do we want to prove here anyway? After all, we don't want to do the work of the police who are looking for the robbers from the Green Vault. We are looking for motives for an accident that we have questioned, although there are no suspicions whatsoever. It could happen that we get lost in all sorts of crazy dead ends. "

"Possibly, Mario. But don't forget, even if it all turns out to be an unfounded, imaginative suspicion, at least we're doing a very special task. With all these questions we give Melanie the opportunity to better deal with the bad events . If it turns out afterwards that it was really just a completely normal accident, then your sister may be more likely to put it away. And by dealing with this topic we prevent Melanie from suppressing everything and having to suffer from the trauma of her past at some point. "

"You are absolutely right again, my darling!" He smiled at her in love. "And I have always wished to take you for a walk here. Unfortunately without Moni, and also without the forest . But as you just said, it is really beautiful here, and many people would give anything to swap places with us . "

Stella looks at the clock. "But now it's time for both of us. Now you have to take care of Melanie again, who must have woken up from her afternoon nap, and I have an appointment with Nadja that I really want to keep. "

Their ways separate at the Augustus Bridge, Stella continues along the main road towards Dresden-

Neustadt. She stops in front of an apartment building and looks at the name tags next to the bells. When she discovered the name N. Kräuter, she pressed the button next to it. A short time later the door opens with a hum, the young woman climbs the stairs and is expected on the first floor by a blonde with a voluptuous figure.

"You are on time," the young woman notes and asks Stella to follow her into the apartment .

"Yes, I hate being late. Okay so you are Nadja Kräuter, and hopefully can tell me a few things about Gregor's life. You can certainly imagine that his widow would like to know everything about him, especially about the last few days when he is said to have slept so little. "

They go into the kitchen, where Nadja has prepared a coffee and Stella pours a cup of the steaming drink. too , we've known each other for at least 10 years. That's a long time."

Stella tells. "Melanie has not known her husband that long, only 3 years, and during that time she has not seen him that often because he has mostly worked. Do you know why he was so sleepy and always wanted to work? That just doesn't get into my head. "

Nadja shrugs her shoulders. "Why do people work a lot? Because they need money? And maybe he liked to work too. At least I think so. He's also been through a lot of moss . Surely his wife liked that too. "

"Oh, money can always be used. Of course, who doesn't like it when someone earns a lot? But didn't he overdo it a bit? Often he didn't get home until midnight. Would you like something like that, Nadja? "

The addressed grins. "I would be proud of a man who works so much, but I think , with me, he would also have to think of other things. That can always influence a woman, right? "

Stella looks at her confused. "How do you mean?"

"As I say it. You can think of something to make the man enjoy being at home. "

Stella dares to venture. "How well did you actually know him ? And how did you feel about each other? Can you tell me that? "

"Why not. At the very beginning, when we met, we had a brief chat. But it didn't matter. It didn't work out particularly well for us either, so it didn't last. But we always had a bit of fun teasing others with it. A few years later, we were always pretending to our other colleagues that we still had something together. Probably some of them gave you something, right? "

"I don't know anything about that. I suspect once that the colleagues do not want to burn their mouths after Gregor's death. One should think about what to say about the deceased. There's an old saying that says that one should only say good things about the dead. If you got along well and teased each other with humor, then you did a great job of turning the affair into a friendship. That sounds great to me. It's just a shame that you couldn't be there yesterday at the memorial service in your father's workshop. It was a very nice memorial hour. "

" Oh yes, I can imagine that! I would have loved to come, but unfortunately I was unable to attend. I hope, however, that I will still have the opportunity to personally express my condolences to Gregor's wife. And besides, to be honest, commemorations like this are always quite emotional. After all, as I told you, Gregor and I had known each other for a long time and were friends. That's it as you can see not that easy. No , but don't think that I was too cowardly. I would have come, for sure. But I was really prevented. But again to your question from earlier. I don't want to say anything bad about my boyfriend either . He was very hardworking, you can tell his wife. Everyone will tell you that. Everyone in the company knows that. "

"Yes, they all said a lot of good things about Gregor. And that's why they gave his widow a big gift of money. An amazingly great gift , your father must have been so generous. The employees don't have that much money, I suspect. "

"That's what I'm in individuals not so informed. I haven't donated anything yet. I wanted to do that separately. Yes, my father probably played a major part in this. After all, Gregor had been with the company for a very long time, so it is only right and fair for his widow to receive some kind of pension. "

Stella takes a sip of coffee. "I think it's very generous from all colleagues and also from your father. But now something completely different. Have you actually heard anything more about the jewel robbery in the Green Vault? There was a rumor that the getaway car once turned up in your father's workshop. Is there anything real about it? "

Nadia shrugs facilitated together. "But now you've scared me. Who started such a rumor? I would have known about that. No, the whole thing is bad enough, and now there are even such bad rumors going on. "

Stella pretends to be carefree. "I also don't know where and when this rumor surfaced, but it got as far as me , and people said that the getaway car had been spray-coated in your workshop."

"That's terrible! That's downright character assassination. My father would never allow that. He earns good money in his company and with his company, he is not dependent on such dodgy and criminal inflows of money. Do you know more about it? "

Stella gives Nadja an innocent look. "Well, the car wasa a golden yellow with a black roof, if I remember it correctly. So a very rare combination of colors. This car is said to have been seen with you in these colors and later left the workshop in a different color. "

"I'm not even informed about that. I don't even know such details. I wasn't particularly interested in the getaway car either. But I think, especially at the time when the robbery happened, all auto repair shops took special care that their companies were kept clean. For God's sake, no! My father could close his shop right away. "

"I don't trust him to do that either," Stella chimes. "And I don't trust anyone in your company to do it, at least not knowingly. But it could also have happened accidentally. Someone had the car overmolded without the employees of your father or himself noticing it. But any other auto company might have done it. It is well known that jewels are priceless. I could already imagine that some small auto repair shop could become weak and get involved for a few million. Or maybe not the boss, but only one or two employees who do it secretly during the night. "

"The robbers definitely don't do that in a public workshop, " claims Nadja. "The robbery was so well prepared that they are certainly much more cautious. If the robbers sprayed the getaway car around , it would be in their own garage or in some old barn far out in the fields. There are still enough of them. "

Stella thinks about it and nods. "I'm sure you're right. When something like this happens, the most impossible rumors quickly arise. People just have so much imagination. And if you get time to think about how many mysteries are shown as a day or a week on television, since one can very well develop imagination and get as some experience. "

Nadja makes a dismissive gesture. "Oh, that's something completely different. The police have already complained that most crime novels are totally utopian. This is really just a fantasy. In reality everything is different. But now I care who told you that. You have to quickly counter such rumors. "

Stella looks mysteriously at Nadja. "When rumors like this get around, it's always stupid. It's always best to invalidate them if you have evidence to the contrary. Surely you always write down all the cars that are processed in your workshop, right? "

"Of course, my father can't afford to blacken anything. But in German case law it is different, there you don't have to prove that you are innocent . The others have to prove that you are guilty. So someone would have to present us with a photo proof that this car was in our workshop. "

"The workshop in which the car was overmolded must have disposed of the paint residue well," Stella suspects. "That would also be an indication. But as long as the police don't suspect a workshop, they won't look anywhere. "

"And my father's workshop has a very good reputation, the police certainly won't just come and turn everything upside down, you can imagine that. Well, I hope they 'll find the whole gang of robbers soon. What a crazy idea to steal this expensive jewelry! You can't just sell something like that. Maybe to some crazy sheikh or a rich Russian billionaire. Who is also might not be afraid to be caught by the German police. "

"I also have no idea what the robbers want to do with it, Nadja. My only hope is that they leave the jewelry and not take it apart. That would be a disaster! Hopefully someone can find traces of the robbers soon before it's too late! "

"Is there anything I can do for you now? I mean, because of Gregor? "

"I don't think you can help me very much either, or can you think of anything else I could say to comfort Melanie?"

"Not at the moment, but we can keep in touch. You will definitely come back when you clear out Gregor and his widow's apartment, "Nadja suspects.

What a strange way of expression! Stella looks confused at the young woman. "If you need a souvenir from him, I could discuss it with Melanie," she suggests.

"Oh no, I don't need that. He wasn't my special friend, just one of many. A good comrade to speak. I don't need a souvenir. "

"All right, it was just an offer. Can I just use your bathroom? "

"Of course. Just around the corner to the right! "Your cell phone makes itself known. "Hello Jurgen! It's nice that you call. Yes, of course I have time. "

Stella quietly walks out of the room and pulls the handle of the room she hopes is the bathroom. But she mixed up the doors and is looking at a large queen bed with a romantic canopy. There's a large photo on the white rococo-style dessert. Stella can't believe her eyes and takes a few steps closer. This cannot be confused, this photo clearly shows Gregor. She quickly leaves the room and this time opens the door to the bathroom, where she first sorts her confused thoughts.

What does that mean? Nadja just said that Gregor no longer had a special role in her life, only that of a good friend, but one of many. Do you put a photo of such a person on the bedside table? Or did she just feel guilty about not coming to the memorial service? No, this photo had a special, lovingly chosen frame. The way you choose it for a very special person.

It could mean that she still loves him. But what if the two of them still had something? Gregor had come home late every evening. Maybe he hadn't been in the workshop every evening? Maybe he had met with Nadja or even visited her.

Stella decides to reveal this secret, but also decides for herself not to tell anyone about this suspicion yet. She leaves the apartment with a brief greeting that she calls Nadja on the phone.

***

16th chapter

After Stella is satisfied at the other morning that Nadja is staying in the company of her father, she studied the apartment house where she visited the day before Hugo's daughter again. This time she rings M. Keller's doorbell with the addition "Caretaker".

An older, plump woman with gray hair opens the door for her and says hello. "Do you have a problem? The apartment, which was in the paper , has unfortunately been rented, if you come to me because of that. Then you can save yourself the trouble of coming in to see me. "

"Many thanks! No, I'm not coming for an apartment. I wanted to see a woman who lives here, but obviously she's not there. I just wanted to bring her a little something, a keepsake from a deceased. "

"A deceased? I only know one person who died here recently. Or is there another tragic death? I only know that Nadja's boyfriend just had an accident. "

Stella nods . "That's exactly what I mean. I wanted to see Nadja Kräuter. I found a nice souvenir for them. "

"That won't comfort her," suspects Ms. Keller. "The two were inseparable. And they wanted to get married soon too. "

"Marry? Did she tell you that herself? "

"Of course. And as a wedding present, he promised her the motorhome in which they always met. But on Saturday , before he died, he was still here with her. "

"Did all the people in the house know that? Were the two a couple in public, Frau Keller? "

"No, only I knew that. It should be kept secret from Nadja's father, the rich company boss, because he didn't like Gregor. Otherwise he would disinherit her, Nadja told me . But don't you know all that? I thought you knew Nadja. You are definitely his ex-wife, this Melanie, aren't you? "

Stella is breathing deeply. "No, I am not. I'm just a messenger and a completely unimportant person in this whole story. "

Frau Keller hits her mouth. "I did not know that. But now I've really got into something . I hope you don't tell anyone what I've told you now. I'm Nadja's only confidante and I'm usually silent like a grave. The whole thing must really not come to Nadja's father. He didn't want his daughter to marry his employee. Can you promise to keep quiet ? "

"I can promise you that I won't tell Nadja's father a word about it. It is none of my business. Why didn't he want Nadja to marry Gregor? He was definitely not a bad person. "

"That was a very tricky story, I couldn't remember it. It had something to do with Gregor's ex-wife. But then I didn't want to keep reminding Nadja of it. Until the day before the terrible accident, it looked like everything was going to be fine. Do you want to wait here for Nadja. "

"No, that will take me too long. I guess that she's definitely at work today. I'll come back another time and bring her this souvenir. But don't tell her about it, it should be a surprise. "

Frau Keller nods. "For sure. You know I can be as silent as a grave. "

Stella says goodbye and rushes to the small ice cream parlor where she has an appointment with Mario.

When she she sees him sitting in a corner, she thinks of the little cafe he told her that there had been another woman. And now she has to find out that his sister's partnership was anything but happy. What a strange world! Are there any fixed, constant things that can be trusted? Are there still partnerships with loyalty? But couples are made up of people, and people make mistakes. Probably life is like that, full of experiences, but also peppered with disappointments.

Mario looks through the window, dreaming something. He hasn't discovered her yet. She looks closely at him, listens to herself, pays attention to her feelings. The way he sits now, he reminds her of the past, when everything was fine with them. Her feelings also remind her of the time when everything was still in order. Of course, he still is, the man who, as if by magic , can evoke all emotions in her. In her inside she hears sound long-forgotten sounds of music. The sounds never unite to form an Sinfo that also makes your heart beat and vibrate clearly. Yes, now she feels it clearly, her love for him is still alive as it was before.

But can I live like that?

At that moment he discovered her and smiles happily at her. He jumps up and hugs her. "Hey was your trip successful? Do you want to tell me something about it now? "

"Yes, because my suspicions have been confirmed. Nadja and Gregor were a couple until just before his death. It doesn't just seem to have been an affair, but also a love story, if I am right now. "

She tells him everything she heard from Frau Keller.

Mario looks at her in disbelief. "I can not believe it. I would never have believed Gregor to do that. I would never have thought that he could pretend to be such a good actor . How could he lie to my sister like that ? ! But in retrospect, it's not at all surprising. Now you also know that he probably didn't work that much every evening . He lived a real double life. Strictly speaking, I now trust him that he didn't always tell the truth in other ways. He may have but these two colleagues observed in anything that has to do with the jewel theft. "

"He always denied it so badly," Stella muses. "But maybe he's involved in it somehow. Maybe he was offered hush money. "

Mario is startled. "Somehow a different connection occurs to me now. These 10,000 euros for my sister are also an incredibly large sum. No normal boss would do that, nor would normal colleagues. What if something went wrong because of the jewel theft? Maybe that's his hush money or his share of anything he knows. "

"Maybe now is the time to go to the police," Stella muses.

Mario orders ice cream for her and himself. "We still don't know enough about that. We should have at least a few clues that can be substantiated. If we went into the workshop unseen, we could actually look around for this paint residue. But if they were smart, they got rid of them a long time ago. On the other hand, this jewelry from the Green Vault has not even appeared again yet. It's probably not even sold by then. What money should Hugo and his people have donated for Gregor? "

"Maybe he is somehow involved, and his death has something to do with the whole thing. And someone now has a guilty conscience and also urged the others to make amends with this large sum."

"We'd have to take a look at Gregor's car to see if it actually had a defect. Maybe Anton really gave him the fast car on purpose because he knows Gregor is a racing driver. And then, at this point where the accident happened, they surprisingly placed something on the road in the curve so that ihe would come off the road. "

Stella shooks her head. "Oh no, we're getting lost in such absurd thoughts again. Look, there were other cars on the road too. Anyone would have noticed if something had been written on the street. And that everything was in order with the car, the police established perfectly. And an expert from the police is incorruptible. "

"That can be assumed. Again and again we come to a dead end . That is sometimes the case when you get stuck on something. Then you quickly overlook something very important. And that seems to be the case with us. What do we have suspicious so far? And how can you put that together so that the individual puzzle pieces become a picture? "

"We have the fact that Gregor is a fraud. Possibly he even fooled both women, maybe even lived a double life. Of course I don't know now whether everything that Nadja claims to the caretaker is true . But there must be some truth to it, otherwise she would definitely not have his photo on the bedside table. And Gregor often saw this Frau Keller with her. But whether that somehow also has a meaning in the case of the jewel robbery, whether there is a connection, or whether Gregor was also involved in something separately , we must look a little further. In any case, the fact is that he had this strange conversation with Anton , which your sister voluntarily overheard . And of course it is also a fact that the jewels were stolen here in Dresden. Another fact is that auto mechanics can also weld, and something has been welded onto the grille of the Green Vault. "

"However, security guards have also been suspected so far, and of course one of them could be a skilled craftsman. These security guards have often learned another profession as well. "

Stella sighs. "In fact, we still know very, very little. Or maybe we're just trying to tie too much together . Just assume that Gregor was a fraud, maybe even worse. Maybe he was a criminal. He definitely lied to your sister and maybe even to Nadja. This can of course be an independent story. And then he may also have been an accomplice or henchman in the jewel theft. Am I right?"

Mario thinks about it. "Yes, maybe we should approach it from this side. I am in favor of bringing Melanie back to your home safely. Benno has offered to take care of her a little. He wrote me today. "

"To you?"

"Yes, it turned out that way. Moni didn't eat anything for one day. But he didn't want you to worry. That's why he only corresponded with me.

And I gave him a few tips on what Moni likes to eat. Today everything is fine again, that's why Benno gave me the green light to talk to you about it. "

Stella threatens him with her finger. "Now you two have secrets too. But I forgive you, you only meant well. Yes, I also believe that it will be better if Melanie comes to my home again. I will also let Silvia know that she and Benno will take care of Melanie a little. And then we'll both go back to Dresden and continue our investigations . Do you agree? "

Mario nods and looks at her smiling. "There is nothing better for me than if I can continue to work with you here. We then have to come up with some plans for how we will proceed with our investigations here, and the city of Bonn is very good for Melanie at the moment, because it is easier for her to forget everything there. This trip

was very upsetting for her, now it's enough stress.
"

"And what happens to the motorhome now? Maybe
we should investigate it more closely. "

"Nadja has surely got her things out secretly,"
guesses Mario. "She's not stupid. And she
definitely wants to cover her tracks. She probably
had a second key too. So we have to take the keys
as quickly as possible and search everything. At the
same time we can empty the apartment of my
sister, may be we find some an indication of
Gregory's double life. "

"Do you think it is possible that Gregor's
committed suicide because he has maneuvered
himself into too much trouble?"

"No, I can't imagine that. Then he would certainly
have left a farewell letter. "

"What if it was a short-circuit act because he hadn't
slept for so many hours?"

"I can't imagine that either. He didn't have any worries, he made enough money. And he had just become a father, the father of a cute little daughter, he don't kill himself. "

"Little Katharina could have made the situation quite complicated for him. And having a child can also be overwhelming for some people. "

Mario shakes his head. "I really don't think so. Gregor had a different way of dealing with his problems. If anything got too much for him, then he drowned his grief in alcohol. And then he always felt pretty good, he built such a small oasis for himself, in which he had no worries for a short time. He was that type of guy . "

"I don't know him enough, practically only from stories. That's why I can't allow myself to judge him. Then I trust you, you have probably already got to know him better together with your sister, Mario. "

"Unfortunately not enough, as you can see, dear Stella. That's why we have to fish a little in the dark now. Let's poke around a bit in his past! "

***

17th chapter

Benno takes Melanie in his arms. "As sorry as I am now that you cried so much. But I also think you held back way too much beforehand. Although all of this is so horrible for you, you were able to cry your grief from your heart with many tears. We're all there for you, Silvia , and I are right here with you , and Stella and Mario think of you a lot in Dresden, they just told me that on the phone. "

She looks at him reproachfully. "Why didn't you tell me that earlier? Perhaps then I would not have tormented and grieved myself so much in all these weeks. "

"We were hoping that you wouldn't find out anytime soon. How could we have known that you would discover everything in Gregor's cell phone so quickly. And to be honest, it was only a suspicion about many corners so far. That Gregor still had an affair with Nadja, I believe , no one really thought that would be possible. You have already suffered so much because of his death, this terrible sudden accident, so we just thought it would be better to spare you a little more suspicion like this. "

"I read the countless messages and all the correspondence between the two of them on my cell phone. It was very painful and very bitter, and I couldn't believe it at first . And the whole thing actually went until a day before his death. How could I be so mistaken about him? I just do not understand."

"You just can't see into people. You showed me the letter, and I have, an impression that he just did not quite knew that everything with Nadja would come out. Most of the love vows in the last few days came from her side, from his side it was already noticeably cooled, I think. Or didn't you notice that? "

"No, I didn't notice. That was just a little less in the last few days, because his thoughts were probably already busy with his little daughter and with the trip to Bonn. And maybe he was also thinking about these colleagues in the workshop because of the jewel theft. I really don't know what to do now. Should I take a look at this Nadja? "

"Please don't do that to yourself, you've suffered enough so far. I think Stella and Mario will definitely meet Nadja in Dresden while they are clearing out the apartment and looking after the mobile home. Just leave it to them, they'll do it! "

"I have such a guilty conscience that you all do so much for me and so neglect everything else. You take care of me and Katharina every day, Silvia visits me every day and helps me wherever she can, and my brother and Stella are so active in Dresden.

How can I make amends for you. Your whole life has gone off the rails, and all because of me. "

"Believe me, we all love to do this. We like you and we enjoy helping you. Please don't worry about that too! You really have enough to do with what life has given you. Shouldn't we take a little walk with Moni and the stroller in the Kottenforst? These walks here in the forest are always balm for the soul. I remember that Stella showed me how much she loves the nature. "

"We can do that, but I'm sad about you too. I have noticed since long ago that you are more than just a friend of Stella. And I can imagine that you also wish for a partnership between you and him. But now you allow her to be with her ex-boyfriend in Dresden all day. You know that he still loves her and that he would like to have her as his partner again. And with her, I'm not exactly sure what the inside of her feelings looks like. Instead of fighting for her, you just let Mario ensnare her. That's horrible! "

"No, Melanie! You really can't force anything in love. Of course, I like Stella a lot, and I was hoping it would develop more, and I also know Stella likes me. But if it turns out that Mario is still her great love, then that's the way it should be, then I'll accept it too. Everything always comes as it should. "

"You see that now very fatalistically. I think you have to fight for her. But what good advice can I give you, I myself lived there without a clue, without noticing what was going on right next to me. "

"No, you definitely don't have to blame yourself, dear Melanie! The way it went on with you, you really could have no idea. There are many men, including women of course, who work very long and hard in the evening. And I think it will definitely turn out that he actually worked many hours in the evening. If you have confidence in your partner, it is not easy to become suspicious. It was certainly a problem that the two had known each other before and were also once a couple. And it was certainly not entirely unimportant that they kept seeing each other in the company. Come over! It's still wonderfully warm outside. We don't even need jackets. Let's go!"

While Melanie puts a jacket and a hat on the baby, Benno puts the dog on a leash and stows the house key in his jacket. Together they leave the apartment and prepare the stroller for the exit in the hallway.

A few minutes later they have left the pine tree path and step into the shady forest, which smells summery and offers than a concert with various voices of forest birds.

Melanie listens to the singing of the feathered journeymen. " You just can't sink into misery with these melodies ," says the young mother. "For me too, going into the forest is almost as solemn as going to church. And although shortly after Gregor's death I was quite angry with God that he took my child's father from me, I still have to thank him again and again for little Katharina, who is a miracle for me. "

"And thank God she is still healthy," agrees Benno. A light wind blows through the leaves, the evening sun winks at them.

"Do you think Gregor loved me ?" Melanie turns to Benno.

"I believe that. Tell me something about your marriage! "

"In fact, we didn't see each other much. In the mornings he only had a cup of coffee at home, in a hurry, and I took breakfast with him. In the company, the employees usually got themselves something to eat at lunchtime, fries with sausages or similar things. When he came home at night , sometimes shortly before midnight, but sometimes afterwards, he usually just fell into bed tired. We just said good night to each other. On Saturdays I also worked until late, at least I think. Or he was with Nadja. We only had Sunday. Then he always slept for a long time . We often drove out to the campsite with the camper. But then he mostly tinkered with it. We almost never had time to talk. And then twice a year he did a little tour with me . During that time he was always quite peaceful. I got the impression that he was always in a hurry, somehow. He needed movement , he was always on the move. He liked traveling around on vacation, he needed something like that. "

"Did he love you? Sorry, you don't have to answer this question for me. "

"Before we were married , yes. But somehow everything was different after the wedding. It was like I was only really interesting to him when he wasn't sure about me. Perhaps he is one of those men who are still the ancient conqueror types. For only something is only interesting that they don't have. After the wedding he suddenly had no time for caresses. "

"Could it be, perhaps, that he was separated from Nadja when he first met you? And maybe he only became interesting for Nadja again when he was married and no longer free? Such behaviors actually exist , are often unconscious and type-dependent. "

"I don't know much about psychology, but you might be right about these theories. I do not know if I want to find it out. Maybe it hurts too much. But then I think again, I have to be clear about everything so that I can really close with him. "

"Are you very angry with him now?"

"Oh yes, I think so. And the worst part is that I can't hold him accountable. I feel like he secretly snuck away and left me with the mess. He doesn't even have to justify himself now and leaves me here alone with my anger. I can't ask why. I can't ask him if he loved me. I can't ask him if he loved Nadja or who he liked more. I have a feeling , that he just crumpled. Not that you think I believe in suicide, no, the police have ruled that out too. They are still puzzling over this strange tearing of the steering wheel. They recreated it and found that it did not happen according to a nodding likely. "

"Yes, I read the report too. They actually searched the street again for traces of animals or the remains of other objects. There was nothing on the street. Only a few lanes in front of and at the scene of the accident from the rescue workers. "

"One day I'll go there myself. There are commissioners who try to put themselves in the shoes of a case like this, on the spot. And then the brilliant idea comes to him. I plan to do something like that when a little time has passed. "

"Right from the start, the police had absolutely no doubt that it was a completely normal accident. Perhaps the scene should have been examined very carefully before the car with the large equipment was recovered from the slope there. Then quite a bit of rubble slipped down, especially during the big storm the day after. Maybe they would have find any trace of an animal. "

"I can't imagine that, Benno. It is not logical. It was a left turn and the abyss was lurking to the right of the sports car . If there had been something on the road in front of the car that he wanted to avoid, then the tracks would still have to be there because there was no collision with anything. The car has been examined, at any rate , what is left of it, and you have the front found there are no traces of animals , no animal hair. "

"Then maybe he was having some kind of hallucination. Maybe because he was so tired he saw something that wasn't there, Melanie. "

"Maybe it was something from the air, a drone or something," the young mother ponders.

"Because of a drone he would certainly not have evaded, not so violently, he was a good driver. A helicopter or other flying object does not fly that low, and there is no area for sailors or hang-gliders. He would certainly not have avoided a large bird so violently. It will probably always remain a mystery. "

Benno sighs. "Yes, that is possible. Unfortunately, some things in life remain a mystery. "

A squirrel scurries up to a tree and makes calm sounds. Melanie and Benno stop and watch the cute little animal.

"It's a shame that Katharina is still so young," says Benno. " She would have fun. I have the feeling that sometimes she looks at Moni. I think such small babies perceive more than we assume. "

"I feel the same way. One can discover something every day, and you learn , to believe in miracles when you can see a miracle growing up. I am always very fascinated and also touched. Sometimes I have to cry when I look at Katharina . "

He lightly strokes her arm. "I can understand that. I hope for you and wish that you are in this difficult time full of grief and full of disappointment and that you still keep your soul and heart open for the experience of seeing a child grow up. "

She looks at him a little uncertainly "Shall I tell you my secret thoughts?"

"Of course, everything is always in good hands with me. You know."

"It's a strange thought. I thought to myself that God took one person from me, but gave another one for it. Gr egor died and Katharina came to me. And when I read in Gregor's cell phone that he was leading a double life, I thought something much worse. God has taken from me the person who has harmed me and given me a person who is like an angel. Are my thoughts terribly bad and angry? "

He gently strokes her arm. "Such thoughts are not unusual, Melanie. I think a lot of people in your situation feel the same way. You don't have be too strict with yourself now, it's a difficult time. There is a lot that you have to process now. There is grief and there is a great deal of disappointment in it. You can't just put it away like that. You have always believed in your marriage, what you have now experienced is shocking to you. And the death of a person is always terrible and difficult to bear, even if it was a person who brought bad luck. He was your husband, Melanie. You have shared a time in life, if only a short one. But it was part of your daily routine. Now you miss him, that's completely normal. And your thoughts about all of that are normal too. "

She smiles gratefully at him. "Well, then I just want to be happy that I have such good friends. I wish that I can be there for you one day as you are now for me. "

"Yes of course. But with your friendship you also give us a lot. You and little Katharina make us so happy. Your daughter is a real sunshine and we are happy that you include us in your life. "

Tears well up in her eyes, full of emotion, she stops and gives him a brief hug. "You see, that's what I mean. Even in this terrible time, God gives me so many good things. "

***

18th chapter

The last guests have left the taproom of the small pub in Dresden - Neustadt. Luise opens the window for ventilation and then pushes a beer in front of Wolfgang. "Maybe you were surprised that I said to you, I have to speak to you afterwards. But I think it's really important. "

"Well, let's go," he says impatiently. "What is so special?"

"It's about Gregor. Is it really true that he had an accident with Anton's car? What did the two had to do with each other? Can you enlighten me there? "

Wolfgang snorts contemptuously. "Oh, leave me alone with that. I have nothing to do with that. It was a private matter between the two of them. As far as I know, the police did not find anything unusual in the car. So if you think Anton might have tampered with the car, then you can forget about it right away. And at the time of the accident, he was in a completely different place. The police have already documented that too. What's all this about?"

"After all, Anton and Gregor were rivals, both were interested in Nadja, your boss's daughter. You don't have to forget that here in the pub you learn a lot when the guests have had a good drink. "

He looks at her angrily. "And now you want to know something else from me. To hell with your nonsense! Always these curious women! What do you mean , in how many partnerships it seems to be the same, but nobody talks about it. Such things are generally secret. Just because Anton can't have Nadja, he won't kill Gregor! "

Luise looks at him mysteriously. "People have been killed for less. And besides, he's still in more dark shops. It has always been like that with you. You don't have to open your mouth that wide, I also know a lot from his past. You know me, even what you do with your car shovel, I don't care. Meanwhile it has also been rumored that Anton was somehow involved in the jewel theft. But you don't want to say something about that either, do you ? "

"I will be careful. I'm not going to burn my mouth. No, you'd better have your beer and stay out of everything! Even if I knew something, I wouldn't tell you about it, otherwise you would still demand money from me. "

She smiles meaningfully. "There are so many rumors. I don't care about anything either, but for a couple of weeks, since Gregor's death, a couple has been sniffing around here in Dresden. They were already with me. But as you know, I don't know anything. "

Wolfgang listens . "A couple? Who is this?"

She laughs out loud. "Aha! Suddenly you wake up. I think if I help you there, you have to be a little kinder to me. Otherwise nothing works. "

He gives her a dirty look. "I don't know much myself. Anton and Gregor weren't really rivals because Anton told Nadja a long time ago that he didn't want anything more from her . It's just too long ago, as that he could be still mad on his colleagues. Anton also loved his sports car, he wouldn't have simply sacrificed it. So you can rule out vengeance or hate from both of them. And if someone had tampered with something on the car, the police would have found it. And the decision to lend the car to his friend came spontaneously with Anton, very shortly before the trip. None of us knew that Gregor was going to Bonn in this car. Gregor probably had a fair amount of residual alcohol in his blood when he drove off. And secure is that he also drove too fast. A lot can happen in a fraction of a second. "

Luise looks searchingly into his eyes. "So you mean it was a normal accident?"

"Yes I think so. Something like that happens. "

"And how about the jewel robbery? Are there any references to your garage? "

"I don't know anything about that. There was once a bit of silly chatter because we have re-sprayed a lot of cars lately. Then somebody found something and started a rumor. It was said, among other things, the getaway car was there. But I don't know about it. This can also have happened to someone privately. That would be far too noticeable in a workshop. "

"Has the police been with you already, Wolli?"

"Of course not! Once they 're, they'll always find something that's wrong. And now tell me something about this strange couple! You should put a stop to that. Who is it?"

"I don't know them either, but they definitely knew that this was Gregor's favorite bar. They were definitely not here for the last time. I'll let you know when they're back. Do you still have your old phone number ? "

Wolfgang grins at her. "Yes, I still have that. You can call me again. Wasn't it nice with us was it? "

"Let's see," she evades. "So you know about it and don't say I didn't warn you!"

"You still don't trust me," he grumbles. "Forget the nonsense! We can revive the old times. "

"You did a lot wrong back then, Wolli. Trust can sometimes be destroyed. You have to be completely honest with me now if this is to happen to us again in the future. And right now I'm trying to believe you, but I'm not entirely sure. I'm still suspicious, you have to understand that. But if it turns out that you are telling me the truth, we can talk about the future again. And if I am to work with you now because of this curious couple, then I need a little more courtesy from you. "

"I'll see what can be done," promises Wolfgang. "Maybe I'll find a nice little present for you. You used to be so happy about that. Would you like that? "

Luise winks at him. "All right then! Let something grow over soon. I'll call you when I hear something from the couple. "

Wolfgang empties the glass in one go, jumps up and leaves the taproom with a "Ciao Ciao".

***

19th chapter

Stella and Mario stand on the viewing platform of the Frauenkirche and look over Dresden's old town, the Elbe with its bridges and the opposite bank of Dresden-Neustadt.

"Isn't that fantastic, up here, this view ?! You feel so close to heaven, "enthuses Stella.

"Yes, and so free," adds Mario. "Here all worries suddenly become as small as the city below us. When we went up here you were very thoughtful. Here in this church, have you thought about your work in the children's church service? "

The young woman smiles. "You cab guess my thoughts. I thought, how nice it should be here in this building to tell the children about God, about his kindness, about his love, but also about people's weaknesses and the possibilities to help them. I look forward to the day when I am in the church on the Venusberg and work with the kids in Bonn. "

"I believe you. But at the moment you're also doing a children's service. We do the work here for little Katharina so that her mother is safe. It's also a kind of worship service. "

Stella suddenly bends over and gives him a kiss on the cheek. "You always say the right words." She smiles mischievously. "No, not always, but right now, and that's what counts. We should live in the moment. And I'm trying to do that right now. After all, it wasn't an easy day here while we were clearing this apartment. Fortunately, some of the furniture is still in good hands. "

"Yes, and under the circumstances I could well understand that Melanie didn't want anything more from this apartment. Do you really want to do it to yourself to talk to this Nadja again? "

She nods eagerly. "Even if Melanie now believes that she can finish with this whole story , I have to ask Nadja again how she feels about this, because she obviously lied to me. Then the last thing we have to do to get to the campsite and the mobile home tomorrow afternoon . I am already looking forward to the return journey in this cozy mobile home. The outward journey on the train was a bit uncomfortable due to the missed connections. "

"I have the feeling that we'll both be going to Dresden again soon. It is now a kind of second home for us. I would also like to take a trip on the paddle steamer with you on the Elbe to Saxon Switzerland. It's still a little dream of mine, "reveals Mario. "Do you feel like doing it?"

"Of course. It's always an experience. We're going to have a little vacation here . Thats our reward for the last few days. Look! The view so clear today! here. Show only what we today s for a good clear v

But now we have to go. Nadja ought to have lunch break right now, so I'll probably meet her at the company. "

The two tear themselves away from the picturesque sight that is presented to them from the platform of the Frauenkirche and slowly climb down the many steps . Once at the bottom, the two of them allow each other a quick look inside and remain solemnly silent for a moment before stepping out into the bright sunlight. They take the tram to Hugo's garage.

Freddy comes towards them. "The boss is not there right now, in case you're looking for him. He just drove to Leipzig for a short time. It will probably take three to four hours before he's back, I guess. "

"Thanks, we're not looking for Hugo," explains Stella. "Tomorrow we we 're going home to Bonn, we just wanted to say goodbye to Nadja."

"Nadja is not there. She took a two week vacation. I'm sorry about that now. I thought you knew that. "

Mario is amazed. "No, we didn't know that. They didn't tell us anything. Is she at home or did she go on vacation ? "

"She is on the campsite in the mobile home."

Stella looks at him with wide eyes. "Oh, Nadja also has a living room? I did not know that. Is it also where Gregor's mobile home is located? "

"Yes, don't you know that ?! Gregor gave Nadja the mobile home. She also has that in writing. "

"I don't think so," protests Stella. "Surely she just made it up. She has yet to prove that to us. We'll go there immediately and sort it out. Is there anything else new here? "

"Well, how to take it. The police were here yesterday doing some routine checkups. It has been a bit hectic here since then. Hugo and Anton and

Wolfgang have all canceled their appointments for today. Hugo also left today because he urgently had to bring something to a customer in Leipzig. But he didn't take anything with him from the material store. It must have been something from the workshop. But at the moment I couldn't even imagine what it was, because there are only things that are no longer new, old, removed spare parts or remnants of paint and varnish. Nothing in the original packaging. And then Anton and Wolfgang signed off very quickly, but did not say where they were going or when they would be back. So today I'm all alone with Henk and have to put most of the customers off. "

"That sounds really strange," says Mario. "I think we'll have a look before we go to Bonn. But now we have to clear up the matter with the mobile home first. "

"Do you really want to take buses and trains the whole way?" Asks Freddy. "You can also take a rental car, the boss will certainly make it cheaper for you . Or, even better, just take my car. It just came here today via TÜV. I usually leave it at home because I only live around the corner from here. I am happy to give it to you. "

Stella looks at Mario questioningly. "Should we take it ?"

"Okay. If Freddy offers us this so nicely, he's doing us a favor. It's okay, then we'll be happy to do it. Many thanks!"

"You can use the car as long as you are still in Dresden. Then it is a little easier for you. If you still have to clarify the matter with the mobile home, it could be that you have to stay a little longer. "

"Hopefully not too long", Stella frowns. "We'll soon have used up all our vacation time. Maybe the whole thing is just a misunderstanding. "

Freddy hands them the key and leads them to the small car.

The two say thank you again, Mario sits down in the driver's seat and enters the address of the campsite in the navigation device, while Stella stows the hand luggage in the back seats.

"Have a good trip and good luck!" Freddy calls after them.

Mario steers the car through the streets towards the southeast , where a short time later they see the campsite in front of them.

After some research, the young man finds a parking space on the forecourt, both of them breathe easy. "At least that works," says Stella. "I thought we had gotten a streak of bad luck after we had these few hours of vacation today in Dresden's historic old town."

"Yes, now we can use a little luck," says Mario.

At the registration, the two find out the location of the motorhome.

"Nadja is here," the man at the information desk knows and shows them the way .

At the very end of the campsite is the well-kept-looking motorhome on one of the long-term parking spaces.

Stella and Mario encourage each other again and smile at each other. .

They find Nadja sitting on a deck chair in front of the camper van with a beer in her hand.

The newcomers greet the young woman in a friendly manner and look into her astonished face.

Nadja looks at Stella "What do you want from me again? Can't I even take a quiet vacation here and enjoy my beer undisturbed? "

"There are still a few things to discuss," Stella begins. "Maybe we can do that quickly. Then we'll leave you alone. "

Nadja moans played. "It's really too annoying. But well, let's go. But hurry up. I want to enjoy my vacation here in peace . "

"Well, then I'll hurry up," Stella promises. "So first I wanted to ask again why you didn't tell me the truth the other day, about you and Gregor and about your relationship?"

"Well, you can probably guess that. I don't tell that every stranger. And for what? That was our private business. If Gregor didn't want to reveal it himself, why should I tell you ?! But what do you want? Now you know that. Now you can rest. We just loved each other. Is that something rare? "

"No of course not. But the whole thing was a pretty big shock for Melanie too. After all, she was pregnant with his baby. "

"Then she should be happy that she has what she wants. For me this is an even bigger shock. He wanted to marry me , and he wanted to live with me. What should I say? I'm all alone now. "

"I believe you have a hard time now. You probably loved Gregor very much. But you also have to understand that his wife loved him very much. It's difficult when a man is loved by two women. You are now just like Melanie. It will probably take you a while to get over the worst of your shock and initial grief. There is also no comfort that can be given. Anyone who believes in God and in the afterlife will find some consolation sooner. "

"I don't know what to believe in. Everything is bad, the people are bad, and life here is not good. Was that all now? Can you finally go away again? "

Mario shook his head. "Unfortunately it wasn't yet. It's about this motorhome. We don't want to throw you out of here right away , but can you please tell us when we can take it with us. Melanie inherited it from her deceased husband and we would like to bring it to her into Bonn as soon as possible. "

Nadja jumps up and looks angry at the two of them. "You must have gone crazy! This motorhome is mine. Gregor gave it to me and we wanted to go on a honeymoon with it. Is Melanie completely freaked out? Now she already has Gregor's child and now she wants to take everything from me. No, that doesn't exist, I won't allow that. "

"You'll have to prove that, dear Nadja!" Stella looks at the young woman seriously. "You know how inheritance usually goes. If there are no children, it all goes to the wife of the deceased. In this case to Melanie and little Katharina. Do you have a deed of gift or some other proof somewhere? "

"I'll bring you the proof. Of course I also have the key that Gregor gave me , but that will certainly not be enough for you . "

Mario nods. "Just as that. He gave you the key cause you have to wait for him sometime. Or maybe , to see to talk after things. But the key is certainly not a proof that the motorhome is yours. Melanie even has two keys from this motorhome. And I think she won't be able to work so well with the little child either. Maybe this mobile home can be rented out, so the young mother could increase her livelihood a little . "

"Gregor would never allow a stranger to live in this mobile home. No, the mobile home is mine , and I stay in it as long as I want . "

"Then we have to get the police now," threatens Mario. "The motorhome will be then certainly confiscate first."

Nadja looks angry at Mario. "Stop! Why is it so hasty ?! You can do that without the police. I just need a little time to bring you proof that the motorhome is mine. "

"What kind of evidence is that?" Asks Stella.

"I have a letter from him in my files at home, everything is in there exactly . And the caretaker knows it too. She is also well informed about everything. She will definitely testify as a witness. We can make a deal. I will stay here in the motorhome until tomorrow , because today I can no longer drive a car. I'll give you the letter tomorrow morning, and we can meet. Then you can read for yourself that this mobile home belongs to me. "

Mario and Stella look at each other and think about it. The young man has an idea. "Well, if you give us all the keys to the motorhome that you have here, you can stay here until tomorrow morning. Of course we will then notify the campsite owner and everyone at the front desk that you are not allowed to leave here . When should we meet at the house with you? "

"Let's say eleven o'clock, by then I should have found the documents, and Ms. Keller is sure to be in the house by then, who can still attest to everything ." She hands Stella the bunch of keys. "I only have one key. The other two has Melanie. "

Mario pocket the key. "Well, a parking claw will probably not be necessary. The others at the campsite will take care that you don't get out somehow. Remember, if you want to run away , we'll send the police after you . You won't get very far with the big mobile here, at least not unseen. "

"Now don't play such a game and don't encourage you! Tomorrow morning you will be smarter, then an apology is due, that is the least. And now finally get out, I've earned my quiet afternoon here and need a little rest. I can't do anything with bourgeois like you are . "She stretches her legs away from her and closes her eyes, raises her face towards the sun and ignores the two of them.

"Now I don't understand the world anymore," Stella remarks as they head towards the exit. "I can't imagine she's telling the truth. It all sounded so confused. And why should Gregor give the motor home to a stranger? "

"I don't think so either," agrees Mario. "It's best if we don't say anything to Melanie yet, she dosn't have to worry her. We will only inform her that we will return to Bonn a little later because we have not finished here in time. Does that work with Moni? Can she do without you for so long? "

"It's already working now. She seems to have got used to Benno and meanwhile also to Melanie and little Katharina. Your sister wrote to me today how much she was amused with Benno about the fact that Moni is constantly watching and watching in front of the cot. My dog seems to have taken your niece to the heart. "

"Well, then we can continue to do our work here ."

He holds her arm so that they could walk together .

***

20th chapter

Melanie sits on the couch with Benno and take a deep breath. "The little one is sleeping very peacefully now . That was an exhausting and exciting day ! Thank you again for visiting the pediatrician with me. I got such a shock when she had this high fever this morning. I thought she had something really bad, but luckily the doctor reassured me. And tonight she has only a slight temperature. I am so happy, Benno. "

"Yes, I'm also glad that she is better again. Babies get a high fever quickly, and sometimes there is nothing bad behind it. An infection, vaccine reaction, or a tooth that heralds a cold. All of this usually passes quickly. I think with a child you keep worrying from day one and that goes on for life, but joy and happiness always make up for it. I think it's so wonderful to watch your little daughter when she conquers the world for herself. Did you think again about the date of the baptism?"He pours her tea and puts the cup in front of her.

"I'm really looking forward to that, Benno. Yes, when Mario and Stella are back, they should be able to live their normal everyday life here for the first time . I thought maybe in eight weeks . Then the little one will be five months old, and I think then she will be so big that you can put this strain on her. So many people in the church the water over their head, could stress Kathi. What do you think about?"

"That's sensible, Melanie. I would also like to give you a meaningful gift as a sponsor. I think all those chains and watches that are usually given as gifts are not so appropriate, on the other hand you only get a short time out of baby clothes. How about a small sum in a savings account, which you can then dispose of as you wish? "

She looks at him, smiling and playing sternly. "Benno, you spoil us! How is this supposed to continue ?! "

His gaze rests on her for a while. "I don't know yet. Let's wait and see for everything. Do you actually want to stay here with Stella, or are you looking for your own apartment? "

"She offered me to stay here for the time being, and I accepted the offer with thanks. At first I feared that she would be disturbed by the baby crying at night, but apparently she has such a deep sleep that she cannot hear Kathi crying . I have to admit, however, that I don't really let her cry for long at night because I feel too sorry when she's hungry or when she seeks any other consolation.

But I think that when Kathi is half a year old, I'll look for my own room somewhere. "

"I'll help you with this," promises Benno. "After all, I have to make sure that my sponsored child is okay. Would you like to watch something to relax or rather listen to music? "

"To be honest, I don't care about that tonight. I was so stressed today, I just need to relax. In which way is unimportant. "

"Do you want to tell me something from the past?" He asks carefully.

"No rather not. Maybe you can turn on some relaxing music and tell me a little bit about your past. "

"If you don't get bored? Well, here are the essentials. My mother raised me alone, and my parents divorced after a short marriage. Instead of my father who is gone abroad , a grandfather had one eye on me, namely a fairly strict, because he thought that every boy needs a rigorous model. My mother and I have a great relationship. Maybe it was my problem for years that we had a very good bond. That's why I idealized the image of women a bit and in the first few years I could n't find a woman who was good enough for me. This mistake , I believe , commit some men. They compare the woman to their mother, and she has to be as good as her.. When I got married I thought I had found the right one. She was a career woman , didn't like children. When she did get pregnant and suffered a miscarriage, she didn't seem to suffer too much. Presumably she suppressed it. But I was very sad. After that everything started to get into a crisis for us and it wasn't long before she found another partner , from whom she soon separated . Our marriage entered another crisis. But we made up again. In fact, she soon got pregnant again, and even from me again. We had a healthy son and I was overjoyed. But soon afterwards she found a new boyfriend and separated from me. And although our son Kevin is usually a nuisance to her, she prevents me from seeing him. She lives in America with him and her new boyfriend. After that I gave up looking for a wife . When you have had several disappointments, one day you begin to protect yourself from another disappointment by avoiding everything. I think I've grown up now. I am also no longer looking for anything, I live consciously every day and wait for what is to come. "

"And then Stella came up to you and I think you'd like to come together with her, don't you."

"Yes, I first came up with this idea when I saw her. Because for the first time I saw that there were other women too. I value her very much, but I don't love her. Quite apart from the fact that it never really sparked with us, I recently realized that her heart is still attached to Mario. "

Melanie sighs. "I think so too. She also told me back then after they met. He was her very big love, something like that cannot simply be erased. I also like my brother very much and know how much he still loves her. I would wish them both that they get back together. Even if I was sorry for you first. "

"It's nice that you thought of me like that. I admit that in the beginning I had to sort out my feelings a bit . That was because by the time I met Stella , my old wounds were just healed and I was ready for new feelings. But independently of Mario, my feelings are not developed in a way that would have been enough for a real relationship. And , to be honest, Stella wouldn't be happy with me either. I'm a person who is pretty simple, calm and honest. I have a normal everyday life and I am quite satisfied, so a woman with a child, a dog maybe that would be enough for me. Stella wants more, she lives her life as an adventure, wants to find herself again and again and give her life a new meaning over and over again. I think if she actually goes to the children's services and is continuing with later her ballet group, then it will not take long , and she needs new fields in which she can grow again. To be honest, we don't really fit together. "

"You will definitely find a nice woman", Melanie comforts him.

"Yes," agrees Benno and looks at her puzzled . "I think life goes its own way. Sometimes you don't have to search, there are fateful encounters. There is an old Asian saying that if you have the patience to wait, you can get anything in life. May I bring you something to nibble on? "

"Thanks, not at the moment. I just close my eyes for a moment to relax a bit. But I think Moni wants something from you. She's already at the door and it won't be long before she'll bring you her leash. "

Benno smiles. " I have to teach her moreof these tricks , you will see how Kathi enjoys it ."

"I can imagine, the two will definitely become good friends. And if you go out for a walk with her now, maybe by chance you will meet a nice woman again. The Venusberg seems to present a lot to you. "

He looks at her lovingly. "Yes, it has to be because of the name. Venus is the Roman goddess of love. I also think that the Venusberg is very fateful for me. "

He attaches the leash to the dog collar and jokes at Melanie again before leaving the room.

***

21. Chapter

At the entrance of the Dresden Zwinger Stella considered the sign of the porcelain museum. "If we come back here, we have to go inside once, Mario. You will be amazed what treasures this museum here. "

They climb a few steps and see the pieces on display in the window, artfully crafted and artistically creatively painted porcelain.

"It's really amazing what treasures are stored here in this museum," says Mario. "Hopefully there won't be robbers here who will steal it."

Stella raises her eyebrows. "I think so. Such fragile goods are not good for a raid. "

They descend again and take a look at the lawn in the courtyard of the kennel.

"I can well imagine how the splendid wedding of August the Strong's son took place back then, and it cost as much as the construction of the kennel, it's hard to believe. 40 days of weddings and big festive events every day. Even a gilded pig was served. "

Mario nods. "Yes, August wasn't thrifty. His Golden Rider over in Neustadt is not made of cardboard either. But he has already left some beautiful things for posterity. What a pity , that we're not able stay longer , but we have to go to the agreed date with Nadja. "

Stella sighs. "You are right . Let's go a step faster. Maybe we can get the whole thing over with now . "

They're walking past the Semperoper, walk a few meters along the Elbe and cross the Augustus Bridge. Then they pass the Golden Rider and follow the main street into the inner part of the district.

Ms. Keller meets them at the entrance to the apartment building, where she is cleaning the front door. "Frau Kräuter is already upstairs," she announced to both of them. "Actually, I should come up with you now, because Nadja said I could testify that Gregor gave her the mobile home . But she must have been wrong, and I'm sorry. I really don't know anything about that. I wasn't there when the two agreed. She's been upstairs for a while now, I'm sure she's looking in her files. It's a stupid thing to have to prove. After all, the two have been a couple for many years. I think if her father had consented to the marriage at the time, they would have been happy together for years. "

"Thank you, Ms. Keller ! Nadja was definitely not very happy when they told her that they did not want to or cannot testify as a witness. But if she has a deed of gift or something like that, then she'll get the mobile too, "Stella suspects.

Only after ringing the doorbell several times does Nadja open the apartment door. "There you are at last! I haven't found a document yet, but I've found this letter. Read it and you will realize how much Gregor loved me and who his real widow is. "

She holds out a letter to Stella that Gregor wrote and that bears a date that is now six years in the past.

"It's private to you, should I really read it in full?" Stella asks carefully.

"Of course, read it to your friend so you can see how much he loved me!"

The young woman reads out loud: "My sweetie, it was so nice with you yesterday, even more beautiful than our first time. Now I am quite sure that we have to fight against your father . I want to marry you because you are the woman of my life.

So that you will believe me, I will also give you my mobile home as a wedding present. You know how much I am attached to it, it is my everything, and you should share happiness with me. I cannot imagine living and traveling with anyone other than you . Sadly I can't give you a ring, because I have not gotten to buy one, so I want to give you a letter which should tell you how much I love you! You can already choose a wedding dress, because our wedding will be in the next few weeks. I kiss you with passion, your Gregor ".

Nadja triumphs. "There you can see it! I should get the mobilehome. I am his bride and he wanted to marry me. "

Mario shook his head and looked at her regretfully. "But Nadja! It's a long time ago. The letter is already 6 years old! Your relationship was broken a long time ago. He has now married Melanie and she has a baby with him. She is his wife, he married her, and that's why she gets the mobile home. "

Nadja protests. "Oh, what nonsense! We stayed together anyway. That with Melanie wasn't love. I don't know what it was with both of them. Maybe she just bewitched him or drove him into this partnership. But he only loved me until he died. That's why I'm his real wife, and now his real widow. And the mobile home is mine. "

Stella shook her head. "Dear Nadja, unfortunately we won't get any further. If you do not have a valid deed of gift, you cannot simply claim the motorhome now. Melanie is married to him before the law, so she now legally owns this motorhome, if you only have this letter, which is so old and can be considered outdated by a court. We have to find a solution now. Is the motorhome still open? "

"I closed the door from the outside so that it snapped shut, the back exit door. All others are locked. Why?"

"We now have to lock the motorhome properly and take all the keys with us. Then you could go to a lawyer and they'll take matters into their own hands. But don't give yourself too much hope if you have nothing more than this letter. But we can also talk to Melanie first. Maybe she has some other idea. "

"Do what you want. Of course I go to a lawyer. And you've ruined my whole vacation now. "

"I can still think of a solution," thinks Mario. "Maybe you can pay my sister's rent and stay there for a few days at the campsite. Should I call her one day? But then you really have to promise us that you won't run off somewhere with the motorhome . "

"I don't pay rent for my own mobile home," protested Melanie.

"If it is decided afterwards that the motorhome should belong to you, then you will get the money back," suggests Stella.

Nadja suddenly starts to cry, and more violent, energetic she pulls them both into the bedroom . She opens the closet and points to a white dress. "Here it is! I bought it straight away. A white wedding dress with lots of rhinestones and glitter, but there are a few small flaws in the front of the top. "

Stella covers her mouth with her hand. "My wedding dress! That's my wedding dress! "

Nadja stops crying. "Do you want everything from me now ?! First you want my mobile home. And now you also want my wedding dress? You must have gone insane. "

Mario calms the young woman down by stroking her shoulder lightly. "No Nadja! Nobody wants to take your wedding dress from you. I only know from a reliable source that Stella has exactly the same wedding dress in her closet. She bought it when we were about to get married. A white wedding dress with small flaws. "

Nadja is startled. "Is that true? And? Didn't you get married? "

"No. I hurt her a lot back then, and since then Stella has only wanted to be friends with me. That's why the wedding dress is still hanging in her closet. And I saw it the other day when I was helping her clear the suitcases. No, your wedding dress will always be a sad memory for you too. Nothing can be changed. "

Nadja dries her tears. "Then leave. Somehow the matter has to be resolved. Talk to Melanie for free. Tonight I'm going to decapitate a bottle of wine with Frau Keller, on her terrace. She is always alone, too, and we will comfort one another. But I don't wait too long, I'll give you a few days, if you can't find a solution, I'll go to the lawyer. "

"I'm very sorry for everything ", Stella now also regrets the young woman, who tries to dry herself more tears. "Somehow a solution will be found. It is always a tragic story when two women love a man. And now you've both lost him, that's even sadder. We'll sort out the matter with the motorhome somehow. Can we leave you alone now? "

"What did you think?! That I cry here all evening? I've cried enough in my life. Now I'm really going for it with Ms. Keller. "

She urges them both out of the bedroom and out the front door.

"A little hurry couldn't hurt !" She calls after them.

Stella took a deep breath as the sunshine greeted her outside. "What a drama! And then the thing with the wedding dress. Do you have an idea how to proceed with the motorhome. "

"No. I have absolutely no idea. We will lock the motorhome now and leave it here for the time being. And then we'll go home tomorrow and discuss everything in peace with Melanie. Is that okay with you? "

She smiled at him. "This is how we do it."

***

22nd chapter

Luise gives Anton and Wolfgang a beer. "You are the last now. And you've already drunk a lot. This is the very last thing to get used to. " As she begins to clean everything up, she hears something, what the two men discuss with each other.

"We shouldn't have done it", throws Wolfgang Anton slurping at his head. "Our beautiful dream of the Dominican Republic has shattered. We gave up on all of that. With the few toads we might get, we can't even go there on vacation. "

"We did the right thing," says Anton. "That thing just got too hot since the police were in our workshop. Even if it was just routine. Now at least the matter is in the hands of professionals. They can sell the stuff a lot better too. Or do you think they'll melt the gold down? "

"Definitely not. They have relationships with the mafia around the world, regardless of whether they are Russian , American or even the Emirates , worldwide . They'll definitely get rid of the jewelry. There are also lovers who pay tons of money for it because they have enough. And they can also afford to buy all of the jewelry. "

"In any case, we are now off the hook," says Anton and takes a long drink. I made a nice sketch of the place where it was found in the barn, but not very true to the original . You will have to look for a while. "

"Did you see the man or was he wearing a mask?" Wolfgang wants to know.

"It was really dark and the man shone a flashlight in my face. I couldn't see him then. And before he was gone, I saw , that he had covered up behind the license plate. He spoke such a strange accent, but it could have been just a pretense to make me foolish.

In any case, I can now breathe a sigh of relief, we are now clean again. We don't have the jewelry, so you can give us not more than arrest the perpetrators. "

"And how did you find this guy?"

"That was the man who has come to the pub and have only given the guard the tip, to make use of the Green Vault."

"Well, now he has , what he wants. And maybe he had suspected that we sell the stuff. But we can't sell the stuff by ourselfs, because we don't have far-reaching connections. "

Anton giggles and empties the glass in one go. "But now I'm curious to see who will find that stuff first. The fence or the police. "

Wolfgang chokes, he coughs, it takes a while before he has recovered. "Why the police?"

Anton laughs loudly and for a long time. "Yes, I sendet the police an anonymous sketch. What do you think. Next to Rothenburgwere so many policemen. I suppose they come with large search parties and maybe also with the SEK. "

Wolfgang opens his eyes. " This is a real bullying prank. But I'm curious about that now . I really have to look at the news today. I want to hear that, I want to see the police find the jewelry we stole. How she finds him without bringing us into contact. "

"Maybe I could have done better. I could have sold the jewelry to the police. Wouldn't that have been an idea too? "

Wolfgang laughs. "You drank too much. You're getting really brave, aren't you? Have you tidied up everything else, removed all traces? "

"You know that. You helped to dispose of the paint residue yourself, to destroy the old cell phones and everything that still had traces of us. Even the clothes we have worn , no longer exists. We did a great job and we can be proud of that. And if we continue doing some reparatios on east cars we maybe could safe some money for the Dominican Republic."

"Right Anton! And when we once again steal something just stuff that we can sell by ourself.". He laughs out loud and do not want to stop and his buddy falls as well into laughter.

"Now everything will be fine, Wolfgang! Maybe something will come of Nadja and me now after all. She was a really hot cat. Although she no longer works in her profession. "

"No longer in her job? She worked in her father's office for ages, and she still does that now. She 's just on vacation."

"Oh nonsense, Wolli! I don't mean that. After all , she used to be a stunt man, or as they say , stunt woman. By then she was already a devil woman. Nothing was too dangerous for her. She jumped on the moving train and down again. She jumped from tall towers , threw herself in front of cars and jumped out of burning cars at the last moment, in the last second, before they exploded or fell down a slope somewhere. Yes, back then, something was really going on with her when she wasn't after this Gregor like a madman.

I'll tell you one thing, Wolfgang, and listen carefully to me! Just watch out in love! It's more dangerous than the plague. Nadja was crazy about Gregor. How possessed! But in the end it didn't work out that way between the two of them. Perhaps he wanted to be a good husband now, a family man. After all, he had a child, so some men become very good types. "

"Nonsense, Anton! I do not think that Gregory would stop beeing in contact with Nadja. Such an affair is also very funny and comfortable. "

"Well , maybe for you. But Gregor? Maybe it was different. "

"We shouldn't care, Anton." He swayed from the chair. "We'll sleep off our intoxication now. Gregor, he's dead. He can't do anything wrong here either. And I bet you that up there in heaven he's giving God a hard time because he's racing through the sky in his racing car and making a hell of a noise. "

He pulls Anton up, arm in arm they sway out the door, slurping and singing.

***

23rd chapter

It is still early in the morning when Stella and Mario arrive the next day at the apartment building in which Nadja Kräuter lives.

Ms. Keller stands in front of the house and looks in disbelief after some cars and a police car that are just leaving.

"Has something happened?" Stella asks the scared-looking woman.

"I really can't believe it. She slept with me like an angel all night and always talked about Gregor in dreams. I have never heard a drunk speak in a dream. When my blessed Eduard was drunk, then he snored or lay as if half fainted. But Nadja always mentioned his name. How did she loved him! "

"Has something happened to her?" Asks Mario sympathetically.

"Oh, it's terrible," groans Frau Keller. "What must the girl have been through to do something so bad!" She wipes a tear from the corner of her eye.

"Somebody gave the police a tip and revealed that Nadja was not only hopelessly in love with Gregor, but also very jealous, especially Melanie and the baby. The police suspect that Gregor broke up an argument with Nadja shortly before his death , probably shortly before he wanted to leave , in the sports car in which he had an accident afterwards. But the police also found out that Nadja used to do very dangerous stunts. She often jumped out of burning cars, that was her specialty. And now they have promised her on the head that she was in the car with Gregor , in Anton's sports car . She didn't even deny it, she just kept saying how much she loved him. Ahead of the curve, they should then deliberate the control panned have and have jumped out of the car. What madness! What a drama! Nobody knows why he took her on the trip! The police think they blackmailed him. And the police think it was a premeditated murder because they borrowed clothes from Gregor before the trip and later sat with them in the car.

For this reason, the police think that they have left no strange traces of themselves. But now they want to examine that more closely. She even wore gloves when she panned the steering wheel. But I can't imagine that it was a cold blooded murder . She didn't plan that long in advance. She was probably in shock when he wanted to part with her, because she just acted as she had to. Why do love always bring terrible things? "

Mario shakes his head. "It was probably not out of love, but out of anger or spontaneous hatred and hurt vanity, maybe also out of fear of being abandoned. Everyone knows these feelings, but many murder because of it. How can she have got away from there so quickly , from the scene of the accident, I mean? "

"Well, disguised as she was, every trucker could take her away unnoticed," Stella suspects. " It was all well thought out. Perhaps she deliberately stood in the rain beforehand, so that her normal clothes got wet and she had a reason to borrow things from Gregor . She must have used some excuse . She's not stupid. "

Frau Keller sobs. "The poor, dear child! We always got along so well. With me it was completely different. Not a dangerous stuntman, but a woman who loves with all her heart. "

"Probably with a bit of obsession," adds Mario. "A real, deep love, on the other hand, can also be very selfless and even sometimes platonic if it has to be. And even do without. "

"It's easy for you to talk! You are a beautiful couple! I can see that by looking at you. But not everyone has a happy partnership . And some , who could be satisfied, can not appreciate it at all . "

"You look a little pale, Ms. Keller," says Stella. "Shall I make you some tea or a coffee?"

"No no! It is okay now. It was just really like a shock. But now I've caught myself. The poor child! They took her with them and will certainly continue to interrogate her at the police station. I often saw in the crime movies. You will say that Nadja did not treat Gregor to any other woman and killed him for that. But I know it wasn't, and I'll testify you to the police too. She just loved him dearly and couldn't be without him. It would certainly have torn her heart apart. "

"It is good, Frau Keller, if you can help her. Then she is not that alone. We'll probably go back today, first to Bonn. And then the motorhome noe belongs to Melanie. We had such good news for Nadja. Melanie wanted to allow her to spend the summer in the mobile home until autumn. But that has now also been done. "

"Oh! That's is sad! Yesterday she brought her wedding dress down to me . Then she put it on and danced in it, a wedding waltz. She imagined Gregor would be there. And then she took a pair of scissors and cut up the dress. She cut the veil and put on a ballet costume. She looked beautiful, like a fairy. She said, "That's all I have left of it now. Gregor and I, we neither belong in this world anymore. Gregory is a ghost and definitely not an angel. And now I'll dance a swan song for him ". Then she danced figures, so sad that I had to cry. "

"Some people have two different sides," says Mario, "and there is good in every person, but there is certainly also a little devil that can grow. She must have cried over the lost love and maybe also over herself because she did something terrible. "

"I'm very sorry for her," explains Ms. Keller. "I knew the good sides in her. She grew up without a mother and the father, this company boss, was always a tough guy. He raised her like a boy, she only grew up with cars. No wonder she did such dangerous things then. "

"She probably wanted to prove something to her father and be praised and recognized by him , with this dangerous job as a stunt woman, I mean, " Stella suspects. "And anyone who buys such a romantic wedding dress probably also has a very sensitive side. She didn't show them to us, but we were strangers too, almost enemies to her. "

A police car rushes by with a loud siren , then it becomes quieter .

"But something is happening all the time," says Stella.

"That is definitely because of the jewels," suspects Ms. Keller. "I read something like that in the newspaper this morning. The police had received such an anonymous tip yesterday. A hint of a place where the jewelry from the jewel robbery should be hidden. But so far they haven't found anything. Probably someone took a joke . I guess the prey has long been somewhere far abroad. They would have been found here long ago. "

Stella frowns. "It's all a big mystery. But at some point everything will come to light. And if it sometimes takes years. It was always the same in big politics, including in America with the murders of politicians. And when it comes to so much money, the professional gangs are definitely involved. They are clever, they have their people for everything. They usually leave the dirty work of henchmen, and eventually they take over everything and turn off the little ones. "

Frau Keller sighs. "Whoever has the jewelry. I think the robbers are not like Robin Hood. They don't give the money to the poor, they make the rich even richer. Therefore, I hope that they will return it. Sometimes there are miracles! Perhaps Augustus the Strong turns around in the grave and appears to them as a ghost, so that they are afraid and their conscience awakens. "

Stella and Mario laugh. "That would be funny," says Stella happily. "But if we can not help you we would say goodbye for now. As long as the mobile home stays here in Dresden for the time being, it is possible that we will see us again soon. Perhaps some things will have been cleared up by then. "

"Thank you for your nice offer! But I've already seen a lot in life, that doesn't bother me either. "

"All the best to you, Ms. Keller!" Wishes Mario. "We'll come back to you then."

The two say goodbye to the older woman, whose face has now slowly returned to its color. They wave to her again and then walk slowly and thoughtfully back towards the Augustus Bridge.

"I wouldn't have thought anything like that," Stella turns to Mario . "What deep feelings can do in a person is incredible. Incredible, but still understandable somewhere. "

He nods and sighs softly . "And with uncontrolled people you have to expect everything," he adds.

***

24th chapter

The first yellow leaves are falling from the trees. Silvia and Stella stroll along the apple alley on the Venusberg and look at the ripe apples on the gnarled trees.

"Now tell me!" Silvia asks her friend. "How was the baptism?"

"We have all been looking forward to it for so long. But then it was even more solemn than we imagined. The children's choir had agreed to sing several songs and a little boy from my children's worship group, Felix, sang a solo for little Kat h i. And whether you believe me or not, she really laughed when she heard him. "

"Oh, I believe you. I also know my companions from kindergarten. The little ones keep surprising us. And what was Benno like, do you think that he and Melanie will become a couple? "

"It was six months ago that these bad things happened, but I think Melanie still needs some time to get over everything. I've already noticed that she cares a lot about Benno. And he says, and he told me himself, that he wishes Melanie would one day discover her heart for him. But he's not pushing her at all, not even now that she has her own little apartment. But they see each other almost every day, and that actually says a lot to me. Strange what happened back then! "

Silvia nods and bends down to pick up a fallen apple. "And yet everything has not been clarified since then. There is still no trace of the jewels, nor of the thieves. Only the death of Gregor has been resolved in such a dramatic way. Can Melanie ever forgive Nadja that she killed her husband? "

"She tries to understand the whole thing, but forgive her? She will certainly not forgive her anytime soon. He was not the perfect husband, but he was, after all, Kathis father. Nadja has now also admitted that he wanted to part with her because of the baby. "

"Benno will definitely be a better father," suspects Silvia. "It is also not certain whether Gregor could really have changed. He was secretly with Nadja throughout his marriage and led a double life. Maybe he would have started this again soon. Some people can change, some not. There is no point in worrying about it, Melanie is sure to look better into the future and not back . "

"Yes, she does that now, more every day . And Benno helps her as much as he can. He's even got her homework that she does a few hours a day. And he also makes sure that she gets around enough so that she doesn't brood too much at home. And Melanie has really settled in here, once a week she goes to the mothers and babies group one morning . She has already made contacts there. "

"So great! And how did the baptism continue? "

"The pastor found very nice words and Kathi didn't even cry when the pastor used lots of water. Later we all went to the Casselsruhe, which Mario then donated as an uncle and brother. There was coffee and cake and a warm buffet. It's really unfortunate that you were on vacation with Jens at the time. Melanie also regretted it, because in the afternoon we all had a lot of fun with Kathi. "

"And what has become of you and Mario now? You've been together so often and so much now. The other day, when you brought the mobile home from Dresden. Have you not come a little closer all the time, haven't? "

"The days in Dresden were very nice, although we still had a lot to do there. We visited Mrs. Keller, went to Gregor's old company, where nothing has changed, and settled some inheritance matters on Melanie's behalf. But Mario and I have always been like good friends to each other. "

"You were in the old company? Have you heard any of those rumors about the jewel theft, Stella? "

"No. The police has also been there a few times, so pure routinely. But nothing was found. So there is still no new knowledge in Dresden. Maybe the time will bring it. Sometimes you have to be patient. But, and you can also ask the police, they unfortunately have far too many unresolved cases. That's just how it is in reality. It's just not everything like in the cinema or in a novel. "

"Yes, you're right," agrees Silvia. "But that you and Mario, that you just walk around like friends, I find that is strange. He says you are his great love, and you always guessed it too. Is there no crackling between you at the moment ? "

"You bet! There is still an extraordinary tension between us, like on the first day. An indescribable attraction and a special feeling of happiness in the heart. "

"And? Why don't you make anything out of it? Have you still not forgiven him? "

"This whole thing with Gregor made a big impression on me, Silvia. I was a little taken out of my idealizing dreams. This earth is not a paradise and Adam and Eve took the serpent with them into this world. I realized that it is better if I forgive Mario. He made a mistake back then. But he has repented and is sorry, and you will surely remember my child gods. That was the topic when I started working with the kids on Sundays . There were many topics for the children to talk to them about. But the subject of forgiveness particularly touched me. I have considered my thoughts that I had written me at the time, I painted also the images. And I have realized that I can and may only teach the children something that I believe in myself, what I feel myself , and what I act on . Yes, Silvia, I see everything in a completely different light now. I have forgiven him. "

"And why are you still not together now? Didn't you talk to him about it again? If you don't tell him, he'll still think you're mad at him. "

Stella shaked her head vigorously. "No, he doesn't think that I'm angry with him. The whole time we were together on the travels, he could see how nice and friendly and polite I was to him. And sometimes even lovingly. "

" Maybe he thought it was friendship? But if you still love him, you have to tell him that! "

"I'm sorry, I can't do that. I feel like Sleeping Beauty, or maybe like Snow White , and I have the

feeling that he has yet to come and kiss me awake.
"

Silvia smiles amused. "You are still asking for all sorts of things from the regions of fairy tales and myths. But don't you have to get ready now for your ballet class? I think , we have already gone a few yards too far. "

Stella looks at the cell phone. "Indeed! I have to hurry. If you like, you can watch it. However, I have a tulle costume that always reminds me a little of Nadja's cut up wedding dress and cut veil. "

"Unfortunately I can't today. Jens wants to do a little bike tour with me in the Kottenforst. But maybe next time. I'll make a note of that in the calendar. Are you practicing again today in Frau von Hüttendorf's apartment ? "

"Yes , that's only a few steps away from my home. And then we perform several times during the Christmas season. In retirement homes, in the community center, but also in the small town theater in Bad Godesberg. There is also a choreography, similar to the dying swan, which always reminds me of Nadja, and which hopefully will have a better life one day. "

"You are too good for this world, Stella. She has to serve her sentence, there is no other way. You must also realize that you have to change. "

Stella smiles. "Which brings us back to the subject of " change " ! And everything starts all over again. Let's surprise each other! "

They take a step faster, they say goodbye at the door to Stella's apartment.

"Then I wish you a lot of fun for the same with the high art", wishes Silvia with a smile and waves happily .

"Yes, have fun at your bikin tour!" the friend replies happily .

A little later, Stella turns to the swan ballet in a very delicate costume in the darkened light .

The melancholy melody makes the young woman's thoughts wander.

This is probably how Nadja " celebrated " the death of her great love . But didn't she also believe in life after death did she? Didn't she also hope to see Gregor again someday and rise with him like the phoenix from the ashes did she?

You don't have to let a great love die. A great love can last forever.

Stella rises from the dull, dying movements and plays the phoenix from the ashes, who rises radiant and turns back to life with boundless joy and full of expectations. Yes, love can always be resurrected.

"Bravo!" Calls the ballet teacher. "This is a brilliant idea! We will include this creation of yours in the choreography. Your lecture was intoxicatingly beautiful. The rebirth of love! "She smiles at Stella and claps her hands .

"Bravo!" Calls out a deep male voice from the background. "It looked , as if a captive in the dark angel fights back to light, full of conviction and a lot of joy."

Mario breaks away from the dark background , rushes towards Stella , takes her in his arms and looks into her eyes , gently kissing her lips , tentatively and questioningly at first , then tenderly and intimately as if in a tumult . A hitherto sealed source of passionate feelings seems to open up in Stella when she returns his kiss. The world around them is becoming less and less important and seems to be disappearing .

They don't hear the voice of Frau von Hüttendorf.

"Break!" The teacher calls out to the others. "Now let's take a break!"

THE END